Yesterday's Yarns

To My Mom & Dad

They just don't come any better.
Thanks seems so inadequate... but thanks.

Dow & Margaret Overcast
1947

Yesterday's Yarns

by

Ken Overcast

BVP

Bear Valley Press

Ken Overcast is available for western entertainment. His award winning delivery and down home connection are a hit with audiences everywhere.

Contact information below.

Cover Painting
H. Steven Oiestad

Rear Cover Photo
Rick Ervin

Illustrated by
Ben Crane

One-Eyed Cowboy Character by
Dave McGee

Library of Congress Catalogue Card Number: 2002091270

First Edition

Third Printing

Printed in Canada

ISBN   0-9718481-0-6

**Bear Valley Press
PO Box 1542
Chinook, Montana 59523
(406) 357-3824
www.kenovercast.com**

Discounts are available for bulk purchases.

"The human race has only one effective weapon, and that is laughter."

Mark Twain (1835-1910)

Photographic Credits

Table of Contents

Introduction

Chapter		Page

By Special Request

Charles E. Morris Photo

Roy Matheson on Honky Tom
Chinook, Montana
1904

Introduction

Welcome to the fire. We're headed on a little ride
through a few stories about the real west. Saddle up
and come on along. We're proud to have you ridin' with
us. There is a different story in nearly every coulee
we'll be crossing, and they vary almost as much as
the landscape itself.

On the one hand, there are true tales of desperate
bad men and their hapless victims; not the contrived
Hollywood variety, but rather a true telling of the
events as they actually happened not that many years
ago. But then on the other hand, there are tales of
questionable origin that have been handed down
through a hundred years of roundup camps. Some of
those contain a great deal of what is affectionately
referred to out this way as B.S. They've been retold at
least a hundred times... just for fun. You'd really have
to get your mind in the right spot to believe even a
single word. Somewhere in between these two
extremes lie stories about real ranch life in the west;
both past and present. Some of them are "ever' word
true", and others.... well you'll just have to make up
your own mind.

The west is full of what the scholars refer to as
"oral tradition". Actually out here we just call them
stories. I knew an old timer who was a master yarn
spinner. He told me that the real secret to a good story
was to embellish it just enough "to make it interestin',
but not so much that it ain't believable. But

what ever you do, **never** let the facts get in the way of a tellin' a good story."

For the most part, I'm not going to tip my hand about which parts might accidentally contain a little B.S., but Chapter One begins with a story about Roy Matheson that is completely historically accurate. At least it's as accurate as we can make it a hundred years after the fact. It's an intriguingly true tale of a real Montana cowboy back when the west was still wild.

On a preceding page is a picture of Roy ridin' a bronc by the name of Honky Tom. (Actually that isn't the horse's real name. As much as I despise political correctness, I took the liberty of changing it to make it a little more socially palatable.)

Perhaps you've already noticed, but the horse is completely airborne. All four feet are off the ground. The scene was the Bear Paw Roundup in Chinook, Montana. The year was 1904. As luck would have it, early day photographer Charles E. Morris captured the classic ride on film. The photo went on to win the photography competition at the World's Fair in St. Louis. The official name of the big event was The Louisiana Purchase Exposition, and it marked the one hundred year anniversary of the Lewis and Clark Expedition. I guess I'm not the first one to find this picture fascinating.

We're going to use the picture of Roy and Honky Tom as a part of each chapter heading, not only because it's a great shot, but because it exemplifies a real story about the real west, and that's what this book is all about.

Enjoy.

Chapter One

The Champion's Last Ride

Just down the Milk River from us about three or four miles is a chunk of land my Grandad always referred to as "The old Matheson place". The Matheson family was of Scottish ancestry, and moved here in 1891, shortly after Jim Hill built the Great Northern Railway. They settled just across the river from Dot Smotherman, near the North Fork railroad siding. Dot was the first of our family to come up this way, and had landed here in 1883.

The Mathesons were industrious hard working people. Their family included a whole house full of kids, and they brought along Grandpa and Grandma as well. Roy was one of the younger ones, being born in 1888, he moved here at the ripe old age of three. He was just a natural with a horse. Some guys just seem to be gifted with both the physical ability to ride the rough ones, and the sixth sense it takes to get along well with the worst of them. Roy was one of the best.

The Matheson boys grew up fast.... most everyone did in those days. They started as horse wranglers for the roundup crews by the time they were ten years old, and gradually got into the horse business themselves. Roy's brother John was wranglin' for the Bear Paw Pool, and was in camp that fateful October mornin' in 1898 when J.C. Baldwin gunned down the chuckwagon cook. (See Chapter Forty One.)

The horse market was booming with the country being settled quite rapidly, and it seemed everyone needed another horse or two. The grass was plentiful and free, and the Matheson brothers ran their herd north of the river up on the range that extended to the Canadian line... or maybe just a little across at times.

Roy's reputation as a cowboy grew. Horses were his life, and he could ride with the best of them. It isn't really clear exactly when the picture of Roy riding "Honky Tom" was taken, but it was more than likely at the Bear Paw Roundup near Chinook, Montana. Charles E. Morris was a local photographer of some reputation, and certainly wasn't going to miss the opportunity to capture a wild Montana ride on film. Honky Tom had the name of bein' a bad one, and for throwing anyone who tried to ride him. As a matter of fact, he had thrown them all.... except Roy.

"I'll ride 'im. Just give me a chance." The bets were on as Roy stepped aboard the raunchy black gelding. It was a classic match, and it was proven again; "There never was a horse that couldn't be rode." The young cowboy rode him to a stand still with what was described as a perfect ride.

Roy was the undisputed champion, Honky Tom went back to the rough string with his reputation soiled, and Charlie Morris had a real winner of a picture on his hands. In the fall of 1904 Mr. Morris made a trip to the World's Fair in St. Louis, Missouri, and entered it into the photography competition. Entitled "The Louisiana Purchase Exposition" the Fair marked the one hundred year anniversary of the Lewis and Clark expedition, and was quite a doin's. Charlie's picture of Roy and Honky Tom won the competition hands down. Roy Matheson was only sixteen years old in 1904 when he was named the undisputed champion. What a start for a dashing young cowboy.

The horse business grew, and as the homesteaders took up more and more of the land north of the Milk, the Matheson brothers were forced to find another piece of range for their growing herd.. Roy found a good chunk of grass south of the Missouri on Crooked Creek. It was about a hundred and thirty five miles from one ranch to the other, but you do what

A horse herd on the Matheson Range circa 1904

you have to do. Roy spent most of his time alone breakin' horses on the Crooked Creek range, and would only ride back home on special occasions.

In the fall of 1914 tragedy struck. Roy was scheduled to be home for Thanksgiving, but didn't show up. His Mom was worried to tears, and immediately suspected the worst. The men folk didn't appear too concerned. It was, after all, a long ride through rough country, with the Missouri River to cross and the badlands to ride through; not an easy ride for even a seasoned hand like Roy. Mrs. Matheson

15

gazed out her kitchen window constantly, keeping an eye out for her son, as Christmas came and went... followed by New Year's Day, with still no sign of Roy.

Right after the first of the year, the Matheson's sent Cal Williams, one of their hands, to see if he could locate him. Communication was a little difficult in those days. Cal braved the Montana winter for a couple of weeks in his search, and found that Roy had left the horse ranch on Crooked Creek south of Rocky Point on the 28th of November to deliver ten or twelve head of horses he had sold to the PN Ranch. The PN boys were to take possession at Roy, Montana, which they did. He told Jim Conelly, the PN cow boss, that he was headed home for Thanksgiving.

When Cal returned home with what he had discovered, the family was now fit to be tied, and Roy's brother John immediately set out to see if he could get to the bottom of the mystery. He also spent two or three weeks in

> "They rode for weeks in the snow and cold.... but still no sign of Roy."

the subzero temperatures and deep snow searching for clues on horseback, but not a sign of Roy could be found. The Missouri Breaks on both sides of the river is as tough a country as you'll find. It was very sparsely settled, and John was in hopes he'd find that Roy had stopped in at one of the ranches down that way. No luck.

Here is where the story takes a strange twist. A trapper by the name of Herman Olson stopped by the Matheson's for a meal and heard the tale of the missing cowboy. Although he didn't say a word at the time, when he ran into John in town a week or so later, he said he had something to show him. He drew a pair of spurs out of his coat; tied together with a piece of twine.

Olson claimed that he'd found them on an island in the Missouri River a month or so before. John recognized them immediately. They were Roy's.

"Why didn't you say somethin' when you were at the house the other day?" Questioned John.

"I didn't think about it at the time," stammered Olson, "but I couldn't help thinkin' about yer Ma and the way her heart was broke.... I just thought I should

The trail was long and the country was tough.

see if maybe they had anything to do with it. I want t' help if I can."

The trapper had drifted in from Dakota a few years before, and didn't have the most savory of reputations, but no amount of questioning or threats of bodily harm could get him to change his story. To thicken the plot even more, Cal Williams ran into a half breed that told him that he'd heard that when Roy started down Armell's Creek on the south side of the Missouri toward the crossing at Cow Island, that he had encountered "a couple o' no-good half breeds that were stealin' some of his horses". Roy had taken

17

the horses back from them and driven them back east
to their rightful range.

Foul play was now suspected more than ever,
and the law was called in. Sheriff James Buckley rode
back south with John Matheson and the trapper to
see if they could dig up any clues. Olson stuck to his
story, and showed the Sheriff where he'd found the
spurs. There wasn't another trace to be found, although
Jack Irwin, an area resident, said he'd "seen a horse
floatin' in the river last fall."

John Matheson, Sr., Roy's Dad, was convinced
the half-breed horse thieves had bushwhacked him.
Some of the evidence certainly pointed to drowning,
but the spurs on the sandbar story just didn't add up.
A drownin' man will seldom take off his spurs, tie them
together, and throw them on a sandbar just before he
dies. On the other hand, if Roy had tied his spurs
together and hung them on the saddle horn, and then
gotten in trouble in deep water, they would have
wound up on the bottom of the river. Steel spurs really
don't float all that well. Chances are pretty good that
someone took them off his boots after he died.

Roy Matheson's body was found floatin' in the
Missouri River around the middle of May. It was a
few miles downstream from where he had intended to
cross. Some of the family made the trip down to identify
him, and the coroner's jury judged the cause of death
as accidental drowning, as there were no signs of
violence.

His Dad was never convinced, and went to his
grave determined that his son had been bushwhacked
by horse thieves. He wrote this entry in the family
Bible: "Roderick Dhu Matheson. Murdered on the
banks of the Missouri River. November 1914."

Roy Matheson was twenty-six years old.... a bad
end for a dang good cowboy. It was indeed....

"The Champion's Last Ride".

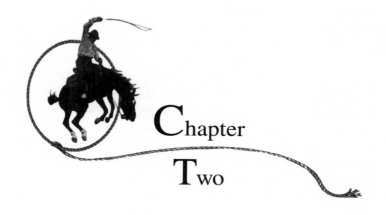

Chapter Two

Prayin' for Yearlin's

Becky is about the cutest little button you've ever seen.... nine years old and a real cowgirl. With her red hair and freckles and the biggest smile in Montana, she's everyone's favorite as well as bein' one heck of a hand with a horse. Her family has been in the cow business in these parts for generations, and it's plainly her intention to carry on the tradition.

Her biggest hero in life is her Grandad. She thinks he hung the moon, and certainly must be the best cowboy that ever lived. She wants to grow up to be just like him..... well, almost. You see, Jack Perkins is a crusty ol' bugger with a soft side that's pretty hard for anyone but Becky to see. They just don't come much more roughshod than ol' Jack.

Our little cowgirl was scheduled to run the barrels in the Little Britches Rodeo in town one Sunday morning a couple of years ago. Everyone was looking

19

forward to it. Becky had been ridin' good, and was turning in some super times. Ol' Grandad had made certain that his little helper was mounted about as well as any gal that age has ever been, and that sure didn't hurt anything.

Becky asked Grandad if he would take her to Cowboy Church before the show on Sunday, and he had reluctantly agreed. If you've never been to a Cowboy Church service, I'd sure like to recommend it. It's the kind of place where even an old renegade like Jack can feel comfortable. Becky's Mom and Dad, as well as Grandma Perkins just couldn't believe he was actually going to go. He'd steadfastly refused their pleas before. I guess he just didn't figure that he needed reformin'.... at least not as much as everyone else thought he did. It was probably Becky's big blue eyes that did the trick. They sure know the way to the old codger's soft spot.

The whole crew rolled into town a little early, unloaded Becky's horse, and started over to the arena where the Cowboy Church was just gettin' underway. Jack had on his best shirt, and even pulled the big chaw out of his cheek before they joined the large group that was already gathering.

There was some pretty fair music playin' and the service was just gettin' underway. Mike was in charge. He's a durn good team roper, as well as a guy that's not too bashful about his faith, so everyone was really looking forward to the doin's. After a couple more songs, Mike stood up in the front, and after a prayer, opened things up for the folks in the audience.

"Does anyone have anything they'd like to share? Have there been any answers to prayer since the last time we got together?"

One by one, several folks stood up to share a few words about their spiritual lives. After a long pregnant silence, Mike stood to resume the service, when suddenly Becky raised her hand, and then started towards the front. Ol' Jack was sure proud of his little cowgirl, but seemed a little anxious about what she might say.

"Yes, Becky. What do you have to share?"

"The Lord answered a prayer for me 'n Grandad just this week."

"Well, tell us about it. I know everyone wants to hear your story."

"We were gatherin' the yearlin's up in the hills, and we just couldn't find 'em all. We rode all day long but we were still about twenty head short, and couldn't find them anyplace. It was gettin' late, and we were gettin' tired, and I told Grandad that Grandma says that God always answers prayer, and that maybe we should pray for the Lord to show us where those yearlin's were."

Jack was gettin' more than a little nervous now, and was fidgeting and lookin' at his boots as Becky went on.

"Well, Grandad said that nuthin' else was workin' so maybe we should give 'er a try. So we got off our horses right there and got down on our knees and asked the Lord to show us where those yearlins' was hidin'."

Jack couldn't decide if he should be proud or embarrassed, but his ears were sure gettin' red. He had no idea just how much his rough-cut ways had impacted his impressionable little sweetie.... but it certainly wasn't long until everyone in the whole place knew.

"I'm here to tell ya, God answers prayer," Becky triumphantly concluded, " 'cause we just finished prayin' and climbed back on our horses and rode over one little hill.... and there them #@%! -*%!$# yearlin's was!"

"Roses is Red
And Violets is Blue
If I just had an eye patch
I could write a book, too"

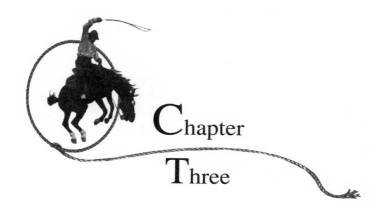

Chapter Three

Super-Duper Oatmeal

I'm really on to something this time. Although I've slowed down a little now, back in my prime I used to get a million dollar scheme about once a week. Some of 'em were real dandys too, but I must be more of an idea man than the kind of feller that can make it all work.

Unfortunately, most of them just stayed in the daydream stage, but this last deal I actually put into practice, and in no time I won't be able to spend all my money. Shoot, maybe I can even keep ranchin' if it turns out like I think it will. I'm going to let you in on a few secrets here, but I'm sure you'll understand why I'll need to hold back just enough information to insure myself some big fat royalty checks.

A rich guy once told me that the way to make big bucks was to take a practice that is used successfully in one industry or business, and apply it in an entirely different one. The logic here is that we all get in a rut, and can't see a different way of doing things.

"First you need to identify a problem that needs solving...... then look in another industry for the answer. Every difficulty has a solution, you just need to look for it."

Now that made sense to me. Let's see.... I need to find a universal problem, one that everyone has, and then find a solution. Well, what sort of problems would an ordinary guy like me have? I really don't need too much. Things are goin' along fairly smooth. Of course the little woman is sort of slowin' down.... she ain't as young as she used to be, and bein' I'm sort of attached to her, I really can't just trade 'er off for a younger one. Besides, she'd beat the dickens out of me with the fryin' pan if I tried that. *That's it!* A universal problem! Every ranch woman I know is slowin' down. If I can just figure out some way to perk the ol' girl up, I'll be able to market my idea like hot cakes.

I was way down on the South end fixin' fence last year when it hit me. The answer! The Vet had been givin' me the sales pitch on this new Super-Dooper mineral stuff he said I needed to start feedin'.

"A lot of problems can be traced back to poor nutrition," he told me, "and this Super-Dooper mineral is absolutely guaranteed to end all the troubles in your cow herd. Your cows will look better, feel better, breed back faster, and last longer. It will put at least six or eight more years of useful life in them."

Why in the dickens didn't I think of that before? After all, a female is a female ain't it? If it would work so good on a female cow kinda critter, why won't it work on female human bein'? Sometimes I even surprise myself with this brilliance. I decided to give it a try the very next mornin'. I got a big heapin' tablespoon of that Super-Dooper stuff and slipped it in Ma's oatmeal when she wasn't lookin'.

"There's something wrong with this oatmeal," she says, "maybe it's old or something."

"It tastes OK to me. It must be your taster."

"It looks sort of funny too... don't you think it tastes funny?"

"Nope, it tastes fine. Maybe you just slept with your mouth open. Go brush yer teeth."

She left the table and brushed her teeth, then sat back down.

"Now it tastes like peppermint."

"I'm tellin' you it's yer taster. The oatmeal's fine."

Well, for obvious reasons, I had to keep the truth from her. It wouldn't be a real test if she knew what I was up to. I kept the dose at about a tablespoon every morning. Anymore might taint the oatmeal even more than a salesman like me could sell. You know, I started noticin' a difference in about a week. She seemed to have a little more energy, and was boundin' out of bed a little earlier than before. I tried including several other secret ingredients in the mixture until I felt we were getting the maximum benefit. In the next six weeks I took at least fifteen years off the old girl, and the results were still improving. It was time for a larger scale test.

"Just a couple more scoops and we'll have 'er"

I found some neighbors that had ol' ladies that looked a little tired....(that didn't take much lookin') and told them about the results I'd had. I swore them to secrecy and gave them a free sample to try, along with the dosage instructions and the list of excuses to use when the oatmeal tasted funny. Things were going great, and I was just fixin' to go commercial with this fantastic new product of mine when a few problems started to surface that have set us back a little. I guess we need to go back and look at the dosage a little closer.

Granny used to say, "If a little will do good, a lot oughta do wonders."

Well, not in this case. Buck Robinson's wife got to wringin' her tail and lookin' over the fence, and then went and ran off with the Schwan man. She always was a little flighty, so I didn't give that too much thought, but unfortunately that wasn't the only surprise. Millie Larson hadn't been feelin' too good, so she stopped in to see Doc Hoon when she was in town to pick up her Social Security check, and I'll be doggoned if she wasn't in the family way. I ain't too sure ol' man Larson ain't gonna kill me. I told him to be careful with that stuff.

Other than that, things are great around here. I've taken at least 25 years off of the little woman already, and she seems to get a little younger ever' day. Just a little more dosage adjustment, and we're on our way to Easy Street. Boy, Ma's really lookin' good.... but the dang heel flies seem to be botherin' her for some reason.

Chapter Four

The Tattood Lady

There are some real advantages to gettin' a little older.... not too many mind you, but there are a few. One of best deals I can think of off hand, is that during the spring social season when all the brandin's take place, I get increasingly delegated to the less physical end of things. I like to think it's because of my vast experience and expertise, and it ain't at all related to the fact I'm a whole lot slower and less coordinated than a few years previous.

It suites me just fine too, and my shins don't seem to get as black and blue as they used to, either. I can be perfectly content in the role of vaccination specialist, or even oyster can guard. One of my real favorites, though is cooler controller. Not just everyone is cut out for that job, and unless you have some very high placed connections in the big house, you probably don't stand a chance of gettin' it.

I get to rope a lot more now, too. Not because I'm gettin' any better, I think it's just because it sorta gets me out of the way. The girls out here even out rope me pretty bad, and that can be sort of hard on a feller with a tender ego like mine. 'Course now that I'm gettin' to rope a little more, who knows, maybe I might even improve.

That leads me to a brandin' at one of the neighbors' last spring. Now this is quite a story, and I swear it's the gospel truth. I ain't even gonna change the names to protect the guilty, 'cause I think maybe the only guilty one was me. However, I am goin' to let a couple of the main characters, for reasons soon to become apparent, remain forever submerged in the river of anonymity. Now, I thought I had cooler controller cinched, 'cause I had an in with the boss. No such luck. There was a guy there that was even sorrier help than me I guess, so they wanted me to rope. That suited me fine, and the Good Lord knows I need the practice.

> "....and by far the best job to get at a brandin' is cooler controller."

I'm draggin' these calves to the fire, and there was a good ground crew keepin' the hard part done in fine fashion. I didn't know everybody there, which really isn't anything new. Another advantage of gettin' a little older... you get to meet new friends everyday. There were a couple of nice lookin' young fillys that I didn't know there among the calf wrestlers, and they were a couple of dang good hands, too. I 'spose they were in their early 20's someplace. One of 'em had on one of those Shania Twain suits....you know, with about a foot of the middle of her stickin' out. It looked real good on 'er, too.

Now, you might already know it, but I'm blind in one eye, and I've got my dear little wife convinced that when I run into one of those little fillys that really require an extra look, that I have to look twice as long just to compute all the information. After all, most fellers look with both eyes. So far I think she's buyin' it, but just between you and me, I can see more than I'm 'spose to with the one I've got left.

I'm draggin' out the calves, and from my perch 16 hands above the dirt, I look down to make sure my horse isn't steppin' on one of the wrestlers. Now I swear I was innocent as a new born babe, but as I look down at that little heifer holdin' the back end of that calf, she's all bent over holdin' that hind leg like her life depends on it, and my one eyeball looks right down the back end of her jeans. You know, right there where that bare spot in that Shania Twain suit is.

On my dyin' day, I'll swear that it was an accident, but there it was plain as day.... a tattoo right smack dab on her...on her...on her...well dang it, on her rear end. I couldn't believe what I saw, so next time, I dang shore looked on purpose. Yup, there it was in all its glory for anyone 16 hands above the earth to see. 'Course bein' the gentleman that I am, I looked the other way every time after that.

We paused for a little break a short time later, and I asked a young feller at the edge of the corral, who that lady was. "The one in the red shirt?" "Nope, the one with the tattoo on her butt." He told me her name, and then asked, "How'd you know she had a tattoo?" I told him, and we had a good chuckle. But, I've been thinkin' ever since....he never did say how he knew.

Fred Olson
"Plowin' Mama's Garden vit Yack 'n Schlippers"
1962

Chapter Five

The Hard Headed Swede

*F*red Olson was one of my favorites.He was already an old man by the time I'd met him, and in spite of the fact that I'd married his prettiest grand-daughter, he didn't seem to hold it against me. I just love hearin' stories from old timers, and Fred had quite a few. He was born in Sweden in the late 1880s, and sailed away to this country alone at the ripe old age of sixteen.

Fred had grown up on a farm back there, but also spent some time in town helping out at his Uncle's brewery. The brewery business had fallen on hard times, and the elder Mr. Olson had to lay off the delivery man and take the additional responsibility upon himself. They would load the delivery wagon early every morning with the heavy barrels of beer, and Uncle would take off down the cobblestone streets, his old horse making a clop, clop, clop sound until they finally got out of earshot. He would leave every day far before daylight, and not return until long after dark. It was Fred's job to mind the store. In addition to keeping the batches brewing on the main floor, he was also in charge of the little bar in the basement, which had an outside entrance to the street.

The hard times had caused the brewery to become delinquent on its business license, and the local law enforcement officer saw a real opportunity. He was a drinker as well as a thinker.

"You vill give me free beer, or I'll turn you in and shut you down."

So every day he was in the basement sloppin' up the free beer. He was a badge heavy, ornery sort of a guy when he was sober, but after a couple of hours worth of free beer, he was nearly unbearable. Beer will do that sometimes, you know. Fred hated the "big bully", but had strict orders from his Uncle to be nice to him.

"Yust give him all da beer he vonts Fred, or he'll close us down."

With Uncle out on the delivery cart, the operation was soon back in the black, and all the taxes that were in arrears were brought up to date. Things were lookin' up. Fred now got some new orders.

"No more free beer for dat fat cop. Our taxes are all paidt. Don't let him push you 'roundt."

The next morning Uncle left on the route, and just like clockwork, here came the trusty officer of the law. He got mad as the dickens when he got turned down. He was used to his preferential treatment, and had come to expect it. Free beer has a way of being addictive, and he was very upset by the new turn of events. Fred stood his ground, and the bully left, but not without threatening to return later.

"I'll get some beer ven I come back, or you're gonna be sorry."

It wasn't too hard to figure what that meant. The

Brandin' at the Olson Ranch in the '60s

cop had a reputation of being both mean and tough. Fred was no slouch. He was a husky kid used to heavy work, but knew he was no match for the bigger and older man. He may have been just a kid, but he had been entrusted with a man's job, and he was determined not to let his Uncle down.

"My only hope vus to get da drop on 'em."

And get the drop on 'em he did. In a couple of hours, here came the bully again. He came swearin' and chargin' down the stairs into the basement like a ragin' bull. Fred grabbed a chunk of stove wood, and stood on a ledge behind the door.

"When he came tru da door, I really let 'im have

it. I knocked 'im on da head yust as hard as I could, an' down he vent. He yust laid dare. I tought I kilt 'im."

Fred's Mother packed him a trunk, and he was on a boat for America the same night. I'm sure there were many tears shed as she kissed her little boy goodbye. She never saw him again. He landed in New York, worked his way to Saint Paul, and wound up in Chinook, Montana just after the turn of the century. He spent the rest of his life ranchin' in the Bear Paw Mountains.

The only other fight he told me about was one he got into with Steve Boyce. They were about the same age and the same size, and both were strong as bulls. It must have been quite a scrap. Although they were good friends, they got into an awful row one night after a game of Whist. Fred had lost the card game. He really didn't find that enjoyable, but that wasn't what pushed him over the edge.

"I didn't mind losin' da game, but he called me a #@&% Norvegian."

The cop? Oh, he had sort of a headache, but he didn't die. It's hard to kill a Swede by hittin' 'em on the head.

Chapter Six

Too Dang Cold

*B*oy it can get cold in this country. The old timers always talk about how cold it was in some obscure year way back when, and then look at you sort of cross eyed hopin' to start an argument. Who knows if they're right or not? I ain't too sure they can remember that far back either. The coldest winter I remember was in '64....I think that was the year. That one set all kinds of records, for what ever that's worth.

The snow got pretty deep too, and bein' the kind and helpful sort, I offered to take care of the chickens while making my rounds outside doin' the chores. Anybody with a lick of sense knows that feedin' chickens is woman's work, but it was awful cold, and even a dang fool like me can see a good opportunity to get some points with the cook. That winter I ran into something that I've never seen happen since.

One morning it was powerful cold, and the poor

old hens were all huddled up together on the roost as I dumped a little wheat in their feeder. There in what was left of yesterday's chicken feed was a sort of reddish, orange-ish, deal that looked kind of like a Popsicle. It was around four or five inches long, and about the size of your little finger.

"What in the dickens is that?" I asked myself. 'Course I didn't know so I didn't get any answer.

I didn't think too much about it, and just picked it out of there and threw it in an old nail keg that was in the corner of the coop. Later in the morning while feedin' the bulls, I found something that looked awfully similar in their trough, except this one was kind of an ugly purple color and a whole lot bigger. This one was about the same size as one of ol' Lars Knutson's mittens....big. I knew better than to ask myself what it was, rememberin' that I'd been ignored last time, so I just picked it up and kept doing the chores. On the way back to the house, I stopped back by the chicken coop to check the water again, and threw that purple deal in the nail keg with the reddish lookin' one.

Man, it was cold. Ever' mornin' it seemed I'd find a couple more of those Popsicle lookin' deals. One in the chicken feeder, and one in the bull trough. I still didn't have a clue what they were, but the nail keg was getting about half full of 'em. Part of the riddle finally got solved one mornin' in the chicken coop. The poor old rooster was standing there with his old legs all spraddled out and his head hangin' down and about six inches of this stuff hangin' out of his mouth and stuck to his bottom lip.

The durn stuff was heavy and he was plumb wore out from draggin' it around. The poor old boy was in awful shape. I finally figured it out. It was frozen cockadoodledoo. It was so dang cold that it had frozen solid as it came out of his mouth. Have you ever tried to break six inches of frozen cockadoodledoo off of a rooster's beak without bustin' his neck? I didn't think so. I'm tellin' you it ain't easy.

It took a while, but we finally got 'er done, and other than chappin' his lips a little, the old boy was none the worse for wear. Deductive reasoning helped me to determine that the purple stuff in the trough must have been frozen bull beller, although I never did actually see any of it stuck on a bull.

A month or so later a terrible thing happened. A big Chinook wind hit in the middle of the night and the temperature changed a hundred degrees so fast it would make your head spin. That frozen cockadoodledoo and bull beller started thawin' out, and there was the awfulest commotion you ever heard coming out of that nail keg in the chicken coop.

I ran to check it out, and there was the rooster, fit to be tied. He was scratchin' on the ground, had his neck feathers all pooched out, and was hopping around just spoilin' for a fight. He thought there was another rooster in that nail keg with all the noise comin' out of it, and he was trying to get him to come out and fight like a man.

Now, I thought that was about the funniest thing I'd ever seen.... but the joke took a sudden turn for the worse. There was this terrible crash, and a mad bull's face came through the north side of the coop, and feathers and chickens and busted boards went flyin' everywhere. I guess the old boy thought his territory had been invaded by a stranger that was trying to take his heifers away, and he must be hidin' in there with all that bellerin' goin' on. I barely got out of there with my life.

We had a nice spring that year. It was a good thing too, because we had to build a whole new chicken coop. There is a good lesson to be learned here, and you may need it sometime. If we get one of those real bad cold spells, and you find some of those Popsicle lookin' deals layin' around, ...remember, it's going to warm up sometime, so be careful about where you store 'em.

Chapter Seven

Raw Roast

*J*ust bein' neighborly can be a real challenge sometimes. One of the great things about livin' out here in the West is that, for the most part, you can count on the neighbors to help out when you get in a jam. I feel sorry for folks in other parts of the country that don't savy what that's all about.

A few years ago Bud and several more of the neighbors went over to help ol' Lester with the spring brandin'. Nobody ever looked forward to that.... it was just one of those things you had to do. Lester's outfit had corrals that were fallin' down and full of manure, and the cattle were just plain wild.

Now, that's not a good combination. They would have been way better off to just try to get the job done out on the prairie someplace, but Lester always had everything planned out, so the rest of the boys just had to make the best of it.

Lester was an old bachelor, and more than just a little off his rocker. To make things even worse, he was extremely "hygienically challenged". His old shack was a real pig pen, with just little trails leadin' around through the junk to get from one spot to another. Nobody ever looked forward to eatin' there, but they all knew that they had to.... it wouldn't be neighborly to turn down his hospitality. Besides, nobody had ever died from eatin' Lester's cookin' that they knew of.

Ever'body got there about the same time, and most everyone wanted to avoid the house at all cost, so they saddled up quick and started out to circle in the cows and calves, and left Bud and one of the other guys to take the vaccine in and get the final battle plan from Lester.

Poor old Lester was lonesome and just wanted to visit. For reasons that were obvious to everyone but him, he didn't get much company, and the brandin' didn't seem nearly as important to him as all the stuff he had stored up to say. The visitors threaded their way through the maze of garbage to the kitchen table, and set some stuff off a couple a chairs to make a place to sit down.

"I ain't sure I'm gonna be here next year," Lester started off without hardly a howdy.

"Yea, they been after me to run fer President, ya know. That Washington D.C. is a real mess ain't it? 'Course if I do, I s'pose I'd need to go on down there to try and straighten the place out, an' the tires on my ol' pickup ain't all that good...." Lester trailed off, lost in his own thoughts as he opened the oven door on the old wood stove and took a seat.

"It must be quite a ways down there, ain't it? ....Washington D.C. I mean. I ain't never been there. You been there? All I know is that it's way down east of Miles City someplace," he continued, strokin' the big tiger striped Tom cat that had jumped up on his lap.

40

The old cat squirmed off his perch and into the oven, and began to feast on the several years worth of dribblin's he knew were inside. Lester seemed oblivious, and continued expounding on the obvious needs of the Presidential office, while at the same time apologetically declaring that he had just made up his mind that Washington would just have to figure out a way to make it without him.

Just then the bawlin' of the cows and calves that the crew had gathered seemed to jolt Ol' Lester back into reality, and he jumped up to take a look out the screen door, allowing the spring loaded oven door to slam shut. He gave a few directions on what needed to be done outside, and told them to just go on ahead and start without him. He'd stay in the house and get the dinner.

"Holy cow we got a good crew ain't we?" He remarked, peering out through the screen," "Tell the boys not to worry about a thing, I've got a big roast to stick in the oven."

Just then the awfulest commotion you ever heard started on the other side of the kitchen. The ol' Tom cat had just figured out he was locked in the oven, and was huntin' a hole. He was a yowlin' and scratchin' and bangin' into the door, and raisin' and awful ruckus.

"That @#%* cat," cussed Ol' Lester as he picked his way threw the junk back to the stove, "he's always gettin' his #@*% rear end stuck in there."

As soon as he saw a crack of daylight, the terrified kitty shot out of the oven like a rocket and streaked right between Bud's legs. The screen door didn't slow him up a bit.

It was the first time the visitors had an opening to say anything. "I'll tell the boys about dinner," Bud grinned, "... but I ain't sure that the roast was quite done."

"How long 'til I can ride your horse, Grandad?"

Chapter Eight

The Cowboy Calculator

We just lost George. He seemed to be fine at bedtime, but he didn't make the night. He had been suffering with respiratory problems for years, and the combination of a hot stressful day's work yesterday, combined with dehydration and a last meal that didn't agree with him, was just more than his old heart could take. We're sure going to miss him.

The little bugger could sure be hard to catch, though. He was the little horse that the grand kids rode around here, and Kale who was nine this summer, was ridin' him yesterday helping his Dad and I gather some cows. Man, it was hot and the old biddies just plain didn't cooperate. We like to rode ourselves plumb to death..... and I guess we did ol' George.

I think he must have been a POA, but we'll never know for sure. He was just the right size for the kids, and gentle as a kitten. He'd been heevy ever since we got him, but no harder than the kids rode him he got by just fine. Last night we didn't get in until about dark:30, and just turned the horses loose in the corral with a bale of hay. I must have gotten a dusty bale by mistake, because it was just more than he could take. Dang it anyway. There are some pretty long faces around here, and I guess ol' Grandad is horse shoppin' again.

Sometimes we take this life we've been blessed with for granted. Some of my favorite memories are ones of ridin' with my Dad and Grandad on some old plug just about George's speed. My first pair of chaps are still out in the barn, and several of the grand kids have outgrown them already. It looks like they'll probably make another couple of generations.

Maybe I think too much. I'm not so sure any of this stuff ever crosses anyone else's mind, but it seems we make a lot of decisions around here based on principle and tradition, and not near so many based on economics. When our forefathers settled this country it wasn't that way. They came because there was opportunity.... pure and simple. They saw a chance to trade a life of hard work for the dream of raisin' a family in the fresh air.

The country was young, the small western communities were bustling, and opportunity was everywhere. They came from far away places with little more than a dream and a strong back. It sure looked to them like there was a better chance to make a few dollars out here in the West than anywhere in the world. They were right.

Nowadays, if a feller made all his decisions based solely on economics, sellin' out to some rich guy from back east would be a shoe in. (If you could find one.) Business people figure a deal they call "return on investment".... but then they only consider the money. For the most part, their family lives are totally separate from whatever business they're in, and if something isn't makin' money, they just quit doin' it.

If you're in agriculture you don't dare calculate like that. We need to apply a whole different set of standards to compute all those assets that most folks don't even recognize. It would take a real bonehead to stay in a business that's losin' money.... but then, there's a whole lot more to life than money. Let me show you a cowboy financial calculation with a few other factors in the equation.

Kale and I were ridin' to pick up an old cow we'd missed in the summer field a few years ago. He was four years old, and we were all by ourselves one fall evenin' the last part of September. It was a clear, calm sixty degrees and not a breath of air. The sun was going down behind the Bear Paw Mountains, and you couldn't have asked for a prettier sunset. There was every shade of red in that sky, framing the lavender and deep purple hills. Wanting to make sure the little man noticed the beauty of nature, I said, "Just look at that beautiful picture the Lord has painted for us, Kale."

He pondered the scene thoughtfully for a moment or two and then answered, "Yea, Grandad. 'Peshly with you and me in it."

The way I figure it, that's a pretty high return on investment. I sure hope the banker's got a cowboy calculator.

 I was headed out ridin'
The little woman got sore
There wasn't no wood in the box anymore
But I took extra time, to explain all the facts
"I'm ridin' the colt, Dear ... ain't takin the ax."

Chapter Nine

The Stay-Dry Swimmin' Suit

*R*udy Bloch was a good ol' boy. He rode the ditch for the Paradise Valley Ditch Company for years, and as is the custom of a good ditch rider, he made his rounds early in the morning. We leased a little place in the Paradise Valley on the main irrigation canal years ago, where we ran a few cows and put up a little hay. Rudy was probably in his 60s someplace, and the little woman and I were fresh married and in our 20s. He was my wife's "Knight in Shining Armor".

It seemed like he was always gettin' her out of some mess. One time she turned the tractor and the harrow too short, and the harrow started climbin' up the rear tractor tire. Those unruly gadgets will do that, you know. Rudy to the rescue. He was strong as a bull, and had things straightened out in nothin' flat.

On another occasion he happened to find her bum lambs in the ditch. They were tryin' their best to stay afloat, but their wool was gettin' soaked up, and they were losin' the battle. 'Course he fished 'em out. We used to have a cold beer for him once in a while. Rudy liked beer, and we liked havin' water when we needed it. It was a real good trade. But there was one time Rudy didn't happen to be on the ditch, and that's the time I wanted to tell you about.

It was July, and the alfalfa needed water. As I went down to the main canal to turn on the head gate, I laid my shovel on the bank. Unfortunately, the ol' bank was a little steeper than I thought, and I watched as my shovel slipped in slow motion down the bank, into the water and disappeared.

A shovel to an irrigator is probably like a favorite putter is to a golfer, or a rope is to a roper, or maybe like your favorite pair of boots. You just can't get along without it, and no other shovel will do. The water was about six feet deep, and though I fished around with a stick for a while.... no luck. I was heart sick.

But, my luck started to improve, because I was right close to the house, and there she was. A real sight for sore eyes. The little woman was out mowin' the lawn and catchin' a few rays in one of those little swimmin' suits. What a deal. I'll just have her jump in the ditch and get my shovel.

Normally she's a real good sport. But my suggestion was met with a less than enthusiastic response.

"That water's deep! I'm gonna drown! Besides, I don't want to get that dirty ditch water all over my new swimmin' suit."

I guess cowboys are just dumb, but I really thought that's what swimmin' suits were for. I finally convinced her to at least come and look at the scene of the incident. I thought if I could get her that far I might eventually talk her into jumpin' in for my shovel. Nothin' doin'. You'd a thought I just asked her to jump into Niagara Falls. She was sure she was gonna die. Then there was the dirty ditch water on the new swimmin' suit issue. I really wasn't gettin' anywhere.

I hated to resort to force, I really did. But if I can catch her, I can usually whup her in a fair fight, and I had her cornered. Our little exchange went something like this.

"You don't have to jump in and get my shovel. I'm gonna throw you in."

"Don't you dare. You'll ruin my new suit." That's the place I got the good idea. You know, like in the funny papers when the little light bulb comes on above the guy's head? Now I've had a few good ideas in my time, but this ranks right up there with the best.

"Well take the durn thing off then. Ain't no sense in wreckin' it."

I just had an idea! I think I'll go lose That durn thing again!

I'll be doggoned if she didn't take it off. There's days when a feller just can do no wrong. Now, she had been in a couple of those bathin' beauty contests, and the only way she looks better than in a swimmin' suit is out of it. I was sittin' on the ditch bank with my arms folded, just takin' in the view, and she was callin' me ever dirty name she could think of.....but, by doggies, it was worth it.

She retrieved the shovel in no time, and was a sputterin' and still referrin' to me in the most uncomplimentary terms. I'm not even sure what some of those words meant. She climbed back up the ditch bank, and was standin' there shiverin' and a swearin', and naked as a J bird. I was still enjoyin' the view, when I turned and looked up the ditch and said, "I wonder what Rudy is doin' comin' down the ditch this time of day?"

If there is anything about that little episode I regret, it was probably that. Of course, Rudy was no where around, and I was merely trying to make light of the moment. You've never seen someone move so fast gettin' back under water in your life.

You know, I think it was a week before she spoke a civil word to me. But.....I still think it was worth it.

Chapter Ten

Kody's Million Dollar Invention

One of the best things about livin' in the country is the neighbors. At least that's how it is in these parts. As I was thankin' one of ours for helpin' me out of a jam not long ago, his answer went somethin' like this.

"I always figured bein' a neighbor meant a little more than just livin' by somebody. Don't think nothin' of it."

Kody was one of the neighbor kids. He's all grown up now, and givin' the girls fits, but it just seems like yesterday he was giving them to me. He lived right up the road from us, and as his Dad had a job in town, he was always over pesterin' us. Kody just might amount to something someday if he doesn't wind up in prison.

The little varmint was almost too smart for his own good. He wasn't big enough for me to get any work out of, but he was always underfoot and askin' what his four year old brain thought were intelligent questions that were in need of an immediate answer.

"How come basket balls are round?" Hey, look! That bull is beatin' up that cow!" "What happens when you turn this little switch?" "**OOOUUCH!!!**" He was a real pain in the neck.

One August afternoon, we were out in front of the shop workin' on some piece of machinery, when guess who comes into the yard. He's makin' quite a racket, pullin an old wagon without any wheels on it. He's got 'er all loaded up with junk he's collected. (Probably from me.) It wouldn't be neighborly not to at least acknowledge his presence. Besides, he was pretty hard to ignore.

"Yer wagon doesn't have any wheels on it, Kody."

"I took 'em off."

"What's all that junk you have in there?" I asked as I do a mental inventory of everything we might have missing.

"This ain't junk! It's my new invention."

His invention consisted of a chunk of sewer pipe about three feet long, a ringer out of an old telephone he'd taken apart, and an assortment of other little gadgets and springs that looked an awful lot like the lawn mower parts that came up missing the week before. This mess was all held together with electrical wire and duct tape. I could see we had a real genius on our hands.

"What's it do?" I asked, as I wondered if our telephone was still in the house.

"It's a shop cleaner," he answered, "Your shop is really junky, and this new invention of mine will clean this place right up."

"How's it work," I asks.

"You just point 'er at the mess, and when the bell rings, she's done."

He then spent several minutes on his belly in the middle of the yard sighting down the sewer pipe until he had it in just the right spot. Naturally, as was usually the case, it was right in the road. We all had a good laugh, and then tripped over the dumb thing for a month or so before finally draggin' it out of the way.

By now it's about the end of September. We had no sooner moved his invention, when here comes the little pest again.

"Hey, who moved my shop cleaner?"

"I did," I answered, "the dumb thing doesn't work. Look, the place is still a big mess."

"Did the bell ring?" he asks.

"No, the bell didn't ring. I'm tellin' ya the thing doesn't work"

Kody Gilge
Inventor

"Sure it works," he answered indignantly, "if the bell didn't ring, she ain't done yet, that's all."

Our little inventor was a little upset with my lack of appreciation, and so he muttered something about adjustments, picked up a couple of hand fulls of tools we've never seen since, and drug it over by the house to fix it. After an hour or so of maintenance, he came back and informed us that he had decided to clean up the yard instead.

Bein' plumb full of cottonwoods, it was covered with at least a good six inches of leaves, and he figured it was a cinch the lady of the place would probably appreciate his help more than I did. After the hour long ritual on his belly sightin' down the sewer pipe again to get it properly positioned, back up the road towards home he went.

Self esteem was never a quality ol' Kody lacked, but after the 50 mile an hour wind we had that night blew all the leaves into North Dakota, he was more convinced than ever that he was really on to something. His only concern was that for some reason the bell didn't ring. The next day he took off up the road draggin' his invention.

"Just got to fix a couple more little deals......I'm gonna be rich."

Chapter Eleven

This New-Fangled Contraption

*M*y miker-wave oven just bit the dust. What a cowboy with his own personal cook is doin' with one of those contraptions in the first place is another story. I'll get to that in a minute.

It was really old anyway. I'd had it for a long time, and it musta been one of the earliest models. It had leather straps on each side to pack it around, and a crank on the top just in case the power went out. I don't think the crank ever worked, but then I couldn't ever get the little woman to crank it so we could check it out.....these modern women.

A guy would have to be a rocket scientist to run this new outfit. The whole front end is covered with little blinky lights and beepy buttons. It looks like the dash board on the space shuttle. Who knows what your 'sposed to do if the power goes out? There isn't even a crank on this new one. I don't think I'll ever figure it out. If Ma croaks I'll starve plumb to death.

What those factories need is a just a regular, ordinary guy to help design the controls. I'm workin' on
a design right now, and when the word gets out, they'll
be fightin' over it. I'll probably be rich by this fall. The
way I look at it, we can get by with just three buttons
and a dial. The buttons will be for the cookin' temperature, and they'll just be labeled warm, hot, and
hotter. The dial will just have three positions too, and
will be for how long you want the stuff to cook.

We could get by with buttons here too, but the
idea is to keep this deal simple. There will be three
little notches carved in the dial; **1.**Not too long, **2.** Quite
a while, and **3.** A long time.

I told you I was on
to somethin'. The only
problem is gonna be
sellin' this to some
miker-wave engi-
neer. We'll probably
have trouble gettin'
him to think up on our
level. I think they go to
school just to learn how to
make stuff confusing.

"Except fer the part I
made up, this is
100% the truth."

The little woman is sorta
glad I can't figure this new one
out. I used the old one for all kinds
of things. It was really good for
warmin' up my gloves and overshoes
when they got left out on the porch, but
where it really came in handy was cookin'
the hot patches on inner tubes. Don't laugh.
It worked good. 'Course everything that came out of it
tasted sorta like rubber for a week or two afterwards.

I got the old one for Father's Day several years
ago. It was a gift from the lady of the house after I got
her a new hay baler for Mother's Day. I guess what
goes around comes around. I still got the best end of
the deal, even though I didn't use it for much other

than heatin' up the overshoes and the other stuff.

She was a durn good hand on that baler too, and with it bein' new it wasn't broke down too much. She was sort of possessive of it (you know how some women can be) and got real sore if somebody else drove it. I threatened her within an inch of her life ever' time she made the bales the wrong length for the wagon. 'Course I never could seem to scare her very bad. By George, she did get to where she made 'em just about right, though.

Time keeps marchin' on, don't it? We lost the baler one of the times we went broke. I ain't sure if we've gone broke one big long time or two or three short ones. I guess it really doesn't matter, but now with the old miker-wave busted, I s'pose you could say this is the end of an era.

She not only got even with me on the first deal, but now I can't even run this new contraption, and she ain't about to show me how. I guess that means she comes out on top.

That must make her the winner.... and I'm stuck with cold overshoes. Boy, I hate that.

"Are you sure all this stuff is the truth, Myrtle?"

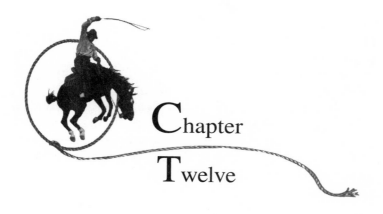

Chapter Twelve

Cow-Pie Alamode

My fiend Barbara is a durn good artist. We've gotten acquainted through some of the shows where she has been displaying her paintings, and I've been playin' a few tunes. She makes her home out in Washington, and like every good artist, is always on the lookout for a new subject. It seems that some of the very best opportunities for a great lookin' picture come at the most inopportune moments. You know, those times when there is neither camera nor pencil and paper to record the event as it is happening. Murphy's Law rides again.

Such was the case for my friend some time back. They were out visiting a neighbor's ranch when her infant toddler daughter got stuck in a big sticky cow pie while wearing her new white Sunday-go-to-meetin' shoes. The picture was priceless, but…. nope, no camera. Mom was filled with regret, but fret as she may, there wasn't a camera within forty miles. The day and the cow pie crisis soon passed, but the scene haunted her for years.

"What a great picture that would make," she said to herself over and over. Creativity is a funny thing. It's sorta like heartburn or maybe chaffin' underwear.... it just won't go away. You just have to carry through with the inspiration until it's a finished product, or it just keeps on a burnin'.

Her torment went on for years, but she had a problem. Although her albums contained tons of pictures, and her mind was overflowing with memories of her little girl, she was frustrated by her lack of knowledge concerning the proper color, consistency, and texture of the great American cow pie. (You've got to be kiddin'. What kind of a sheltered life has this gal lived?) Apparently her experience with "Ye Olde Meadow Muffin" has not been the same as that of the girls in the circles in which I travel. Most of them have had extensive and all too intimate contact with the "Perfume of the Plains".

A good artist wants the final picture to be just right, so there was only one thing to do.... **BORROW ONE**. There was a big registered cow outfit down the road a ways, so Barbara gives them a call.

"You want to borrow what?" the incredulous ranch manager asked. "Louie, we've got ourselves a real fruit cake here," he laughed to one of the hands under his breath.

She went on to explain further who she was, and what she needed.

"You gotta be kiddin', lady. I've worked here for thirty five years and I've never heard tell of a deal like this before. This beats anything I ever heard. What do you need a real one for? Can't you just get some greenish brown paint and paint the durn thing?"

Barbara went on to explain that although they had horses at their place, they didn't have any cows,

60

and she wanted the picture to be just right.

"Yes Ma'am. I think I understand. You just come on over and we'll see if we can help," the ranch manager laughed.

How to carry it home without disturbing it's natural shape and original state presented a real problem, but this gal is a real thinker.

"I know! I'll just get the big flat shovel out of the garage, and scoop it up very carefully and put it in the trunk. Then if I drive really slow on the way home, it should get here just perfectly."

About a half an hour later the boys at the ranch looked up just as the big Caddy came cruisin' down the lane. This wasn't the first luxury car this outfit had ever seen. The ranch was owned by a group of investors from the east coast, and sold high dollar breeding stock all over the world. They took their new lady visitor to the pasture near the barn to find just the perfect cow pie, and had a good laugh as she seemed so intent on getting just the right one. None seemed to be exactly what she was looking for. They were either too dry, or they wouldn't stick together well enough for the ride home. Finally they decided to look in the barn..... and there it was! The perfect cow pie! Barbara appreciatively and carefully scooped it up, and even offered to pay for it. The boys laughed, declined payment, and went out the back of the barn as she exited the front door. Just as she was loadin' the shovel and its precious cargo into the Caddy's trunk, who should drive up, but some Arabian visitors that were prospective customers for the ranch's high dollar heifers. Barbara just couldn't resist.

"We're just cleaning up a little so the barn would look nice when you got here."

The oil sheiks were obviously impressed. After all, they *were* very important. Barbara slammed the trunk and giggled all the way home.

Though it's common knowlege out here on the plains
Some may not know, so let me explain
The males of the species are boss.... so they think
But they're scared of a girl with her tail in a kink

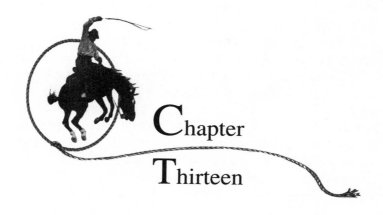

Chapter Thirteen

Good Friends, Bad Booze
And a Dead Man

I've always gotten along well with crusty old codgers that everyone else seems to avoid. It just could be we have more in common than I'd like to admit. The stories of the old days can hold me in suspense for hours. The old buzzards seem to kinda take a likin' to me, too.... maybe it's because I'm the only one that'll listen. One of my old crony pals was in a mood to visit this week and really told me a dandy.

"My old Grandad always told me a man should be like a good horse.... keep his mouth shut, but I figure I can trust you. 'Sides, nobody believes anything you say anyhow." He laughed, spit out a big wad of snoose, and began his story. Because I know some of the relatives of the parties involved here, I've taken the liberty of changing the names. My source, of course, must remain anonymous.

It was back in the thirties during the Great Depression. (It's called Great to differentiate it from just our ordinary annually recurring depression.) Prohibition was in force and the country was swarmin' with U.S. Revenue Agents. They were trying, mostly in vain, to stop the illegal importation and manufacture of booze.

To say they weren't all that popular with a lot of folks around this neck of the woods would be an understatement. The coulees outnumbered the moonshine stills in these parts, but just barely. Human nature is a funny thing. Go ahead and try telling someone they can't do somethin' they've been doing for years, because Congress has recently passed a law for their own good.... and now it's illegal. Big deal.

Watson was a Revenue man. He was young and dashing and quite captivated with a certain young lady he'd met on one of their mutual visits to our fair little city. The young lady was also noticeably interested in him, and was greatly enjoying the attention he afforded her. Unfortunately, her father did not agree with her obvious lack of judgment.

It's easy to get "lost" in the Missouri Breaks.

"I'd rather see you get hooked up with a horse thief." That could have had something to do with the fact that ol' Dad was a first rate cowboy, and had been suspected of tradin' a few horses not strictly his own on occasion. He put the run on Watson, and told him not to bother coming back.

It was during the holiday season around New Years and ol' Dad hosted a big party at the ranch on the south side of the Bear Paws. As parties tended to do in those times, it went 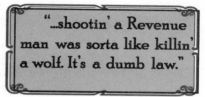 on for a couple of days, with dancing and feasting and not just a little "shine" to encourage the guests in their celebration.

Who should show up but Mr. Watson, the Revenue Man. He called ol' Dad outside, and asked him about the spirits that he and his guests had been so freely enjoying.

"I'm just showin' my friends a good time."

"That's not legal, and you know it."

"I ain't sellin' it, and **YOU** know it. You're just sore 'cause I won't let you carry on with Annie."

"Mr. Widman (not really his name), I'm placing you under arrest for the illegal possession of liquor."

"Oh, yea?"

The fight was on. Watson was younger, but ol' Dad was a real scrapper. One thing led to another. Watson went for his gun, but was too slow, and wound up with two 45 slugs near his heart. Some of the guests, including my old confidant, helped ol' Dad drag the body into the root cellar.... ironically right next to the moonshine still, and the party continued until the next morning.

What we need to understand is that although the killin' was technically a crime, the predominate view in that camp was that it definitely shouldn't be looked upon as murder. In spite of the fact that the long arm of the law was certain to see things differently, the victim was after all, just a Revenue Man.

It would be more like us shootin' a wolf that's eatin' our livestock. Sure it's against the law.... but it's a dumb law. You do what you've gotta do.

The next morning the effects of the spirits had worn off some, and the reality of the situation started to sink in. They had a body and a car to deal with. Poor old Watson's carcass was unceremoniously carried down a coulee in the Missouri Breaks, and placed under a big cut bank that was caved off to cover the remains. The car was also taken down the trail to the Missouri River with the aid of a couple of teams of horses. A big hole was chopped in the ice in the deepest portion of the river and the car shoved in. Within a few minutes, all that remained was the hole, and at twenty below zero, that was pretty well fixed in a couple of hours. The next evening a fresh snowfall covered the rest of the tracks.

Everyone lost. The Revenue folks lost a good zealous agent, Annie lost a suitor, ol' Dad was out a couple of good bullets, and poor old Watson lost his life.

If Widman had a conscience, it was sure to have gotten sore a time or two, but he definitely had some faithful friends. It took 70 years for one of 'em to talk.

Chapter Fourteen

The Skeeters in '78

The skeeters sure can get thick up here in the summer time. We need to get some of those "Be Kind to Critters" folks to put on their swimmin' suits and come along to help change the irrigatin' water just before dark. They might just have a change of heart....that is, if they lived through it. I heard that in some of the parks up in Canada that they've plumb quit sprayin' them. They want the place to be "a' naturale". That should help with the over-crowded campgrounds.

They're pretty good sized this year, too, although not nearly as big as they were in '78. I think that must have been a record. I never will forget that year. I've been awful hesitant tellin' this story, because nobody would believe it anyway, and didn't want to waste the air. Then just yesterday I ran into an ol' boy that had the same thing happen to him, so it's time to come clean.

It was along about the first of August sometime, things were busy as usual, and the little woman hadn't gotten around to shuttin' up her chickens until it was nearly dark. The coons are pretty bad up here on the river, and you have to shut that door every night or sure as the world somethin' will get in and kill a bunch of them. She had just gotten to the coop, and because it was almost dark, she didn't even see that big ol' skeeter in there standin' on the feeder and peckin' at the wheat.

I was right behind her, and I saw him all right, but it was too late. When that door slammed shut he came plumb unwound. They can get awful wild when they get cornered. He started flyin' around in there and bumpin' into the door and the chicken wire on the window, but couldn't find a way out. We were afraid to open the door, as riled up as he was, and because of the danger, we decided to just wait until mornin'. I figured to sneak out about daylight after he'd had time to cool down a little, and slip the door back open.

I was there before sun up, and quiet as a mouse, slowly opened the door. Out he came. Luckily I was standin' to the side, and he just barely missed me as he roared past. I've seen some skeeters in my time, but that was beyond a doubt the biggest one I'd ever encountered. I really wasn't lookin' forward to going in to check out the damage.

The place was a real mess. There were feathers everywhere, and the poor ol' chickens were all huddled together and scared plumb to death. That's when I saw the real catastrophe. We had a pair of turkeys we'd been keepin' in the coop too, and the poor old Tom was deader than a mackerel. It looked like he'd taken an awful whuppin'.

I buried the old boy before breakfast, and it was a few days before we pieced the whole story together. It soon became apparent to even the most casual observer that the hen turkey was in the family way, and when the eggs started hatchin' our suspicions were confirmed. Yup, he did. If anyone tells you it can't happen, they don't know what they're talkin' about.

They were sort of strange lookin' little critters. They didn't have much for feathers, and they were kind of feisty, but if you just left 'em alone you could get along OK. We did have to clip their wings a couple of times to keep 'em from flyin' over the fence, and they were sort of bad to peck, but other than that, they weren't much trouble.

They got about the size of a Leghorn rooster by the time they were ready to butcher, and gettin' them caught and killed really wasn't all that easy. We had to use a sheep hook to snag 'em off of the roost at night, and with one guy standin' on their beak, the other one used the ax. They were a little tough to hold down, and in the excitement, I cut a toe plumb off of one of Lester Thompson's boots. It turned out all right though, because thank Goodness I completely missed his toes.

"I was never so scared in my whole life!"

The pin feathers were the some of the worst I've ever seen, but after we finally got them picked, they really didn't taste all that bad. You just about had to boil 'em, though.... the durn things were awful tough. The skeeters ain't near that big this summer, and I sure hope I never see another year like '78.

"Let's get outa here, Clarabelle! It's gettin'
so deep a girl could drown in this stuff."

Chapter Fifteen

The Famous El-Dorado Massage

I'm sure you've heard it said that you can take the boy out of the country, but they can't ever seem to get the country out of the boy. There's another slant to that little deal. For anyone who has spent a lot of time on a horse.... just gettin' done what needs to be done in the cow business, there are a few necessary adjustments that need to be made to properly function in the rest of motorized society.

Some ol' boys just seem to have a heck of a time making the transition. It isn't nearly as dramatic as the change that Grandad had to make, having never driven an outfit with an engine before, but they none the less seem to keep forgettin' they're not still horseback. They're used to just pullin' their hat down and gettin' the job done without giving a second thought to life, limb, or the wear and tear on man and beast. After all, the job needs doin' and he's going to get 'er done or die tryin'. Besides, things usually turn out all right in the end.... don't they?

I know a lot of them that just continue to drive like their ridin', and these dang four wheel drive pickups certainly haven't helped the transition much. They aren't as bad to get stuck or high centered as the old two wheel types, and I think they've greatly contributed to encouragin' the old buckaroos to just keep doin' things like they have been. If they'd get hung up a little more often, they just might be convinced to change their ways.

You'll notice that most of the four wheel drive outfits that cowboys drive are sportin' a dilapidated grill guard....usually pretty badly bent up, with various colors of fuzz dangling from it. Upon closer inspection, you will find that the most recent fuzz deposit was formerly, and probably quite recently, attached to the reluctant north end of a bull that was being gently persuaded to go back further south where he belonged.

Years ago when an easterner was appalled by the way the Montana cowboys were carrying on, and accused them of being "totally wild and completely untamed", Charlie Russell set him straight.

"They ain't either. I know for a fact that they're part human." A lot of things have changed in the last hundred years, but the "modus operande" of the cowboy really hasn't.

Clyde (alias "Crash") Morgan sort of operates like that. His poor old pickup even looks worse than mine.... and that's really saying something. His ol' lady had been chewin' on his tail for years to get her a little nicer outfit to go to town in. The doors on the old pickup she had to drive were either stuck shut or floppin' open, dependin' on their mood, and the rest of it went down hill from there.

This spring everything changed.... at least temporarily. The Morgan outfit wintered their calves over this past year and after selling them for a big price about the first of May, the little woman was ridin' ol' Clyde pretty hard for a new car. He delivered the high priced steers, then went straight down to the Mint to celebrate the great stroke of business.

As fate would have it, after a prolonged period of copious consumption of illicit liquids, he ran into Fast Eddy, the Cadillac dealer. The sale was a breeze. Fast Eddy had him fixed up in no time, and even offered to drive his old pickup back out to the ranch for him.

Clyde slapped back a couple more for the road, and then started home in his shiny new beauty. She had white wall tires.... the very first ones on the ranch, and some of those high-dollar spoke wheels. You could even see your teeth in that fancy paint job. Little did ol' Crash know, that all that new fancy would be short lived. Just as he was turnin' off the county road, I'll be dad-blamed if one of those ropin' steers that the neighbors had just brought up from Mexico wasn't in with his purebred heifers. The trouble was this one wasn't a steer.... yet, and he seemed to have a great deal of affection for a couple of the ladies gracing his company.

It probably won't take a rocket scientist to figure what happened next. Crash got his tail in a knot, and was determined to show their uninvited guest the door. Through the gate and into the herd flew the Cadillac cowboy, and in the heat of battle just couldn't resist administering an El Dorado massage to the south end of this would be "Latin Lover".

The front of that brand new Caddy unfortunately doesn't look quite the same as it did.... but By George the bull went home. Some guys should just stay horseback.

Anybody know where to get a grill guard for a Cadillac?

Chapter Sixteen

Leadin' the Herd

I'm a lucky guy. Some wise old fella once said that life is just a series of choices, and we sort of plan our own destiny. Well, I ain't sure about you, but some of the most important things that have helped to shape who I am, I didn't have a durn thing to do with.

They say you can pick your friends, but you're stuck with your relatives. That really isn't a problem in my case, 'cause just by chance I guess, I was lucky enough to land in a hard workin', God fearing, honest family of country folks smack in the middle of Montana. I'd like to take a little of the credit for that, but I'm havin' a hard time figuring out how. Heck, I'm havin' a hard time just living up to the reputation that was handed to me for free. Let me tell you a little story about the kind of guy my Dad is.

First, I need to give you a little background information. In the late 50's sometime, one of the biggest ranches in Montana was liquidated. The Miller Brothers were reported to own the second largest privately held ranch in the state, and they sold their extensive operation to Wellington D. Rankin.

The Millers were real managers, and ran a tight ship. Mr. Rankin, on the other hand, was a lawyer, and a pretty sharp cookie. The Millers had spent 75 years or so putting this operation together, and had every reason to be very proud of what they'd gotten done. They understandably wanted to sell it in one chunk, to keep the ranch intact. They were thinkin' like ranchers. Mr. Rankin saw a real opportunity, and was thinkin' like a lawyer.

To make a long story a little shorter, the once proud and efficient ranch was raped by mismanagement and lack of manpower. There were a few good people workin' there, but they couldn't start to keep up with what had to be done. Mr. Rankin got a lot of his help from the State Prison in Deer Lodge. In order to be eligible for parole, the inmates there needed a job to go to, and Mr. Rankin provided one. I doubt if he paid all that well, and many of the guys that did amount to something didn't know "sic 'um" about a cow. It was a real disaster.

Dad's first Sunday Suit

It may have begun innocently, (who's to say?) but when the big bunches of cattle were moved, there were

My Dad & Grandad in the '40s

Dow Overcast, Jr. & Dow Overcast, Sr.
"A couple of workin' fools."

orphan calves everywhere. The calves would lose track of their Ma, and would head back to where they sucked last. Either out of neglect, lack of man power, or just plain stupidity, the cattle were never mothered up after the move.

The little buggers were gonna die unless someone fed 'em, and the new "lawyer turned rancher" hadn't exactly endeared himself to his neighbors. Pickin' up some of "Rankin's bums" became rather routine in more than one cow camp around here. Unfortunately, free calves (like free booze) often leads to excess. Some of the more ambitious cowboys didn't bother waitin' for the slick calves to lose track of their mothers, and began to help them along in the weanin' process. The problem got to be epidemic.

If you ranched in Blaine County you either bordered Rankin land, or it wasn't far down the road, and our summer range was no exception. One fall in the early 60's a Rankin cow bearing the old Miller Brother's E Bar Y brand showed up in our bunch. She was a big good lookin' Hereford cow with a pair of slick black baldy calves that weighed about 300 pounds.

I was just in my early teens with more pimples than brains, and was all ears as I listened to Dad and the other men decidin' what to do with our new strays. It really wouldn't have taken much imagination to justify keeping the calves and dumpin' the cow back in one of the Rankin pastures. Dad turned and looked at me and my little brothers and said, "I guess we'd better call the brand inspector."

The brand man drove in the yard, and nearly had a heart attack. He really couldn't believe Dad had called him......here is someone actually trying to get rid of slick Rankin calves.

It's been said that the whole Rankin ranchin' fiasco made thieves out of good honest men. I won't debate that, but I know one good honest man that didn't take the bait.

I've heard him relate this old story a few times, and Dad always says, "I really wanted to keep those calves, but the boys were watchin'."

I really don't think that keeping them ever seriously crossed his mind..... but the boys *were* watchin'. Thanks Dad. I hope we can pass on what you passed us.

Chapter Seventeen

A Dang Snakey Preacher

*H*ot weather sure can make the snakes cranky. When the air is cool they get pretty slow, but when she's hot it's a different deal. Boy, I hate snakes. The only good one is a dead one as far as I'm concerned.....I don't care what kind it is.

For the sheltered and uneducated among us, I should probably give a rudimentary lesson on the proper method of snake killin'. If you keep your eyes pealed, they really aren't too hard to spot on the county road in these parts, and unless you have your technique perfected, they'll get away and live to scare the pants off of someone else. The secret is to lock up all the brakes and skid right through the middle of 'em. That will get them every time, and leads me to a true story that needs tellin'.

I needed to visit with one of the neighbors about something not long ago, and saw his swather running up by the road, so I waited until it came around again.

The door opened, and his wife stepped out. I know that in ranch country seein' the lady of the house on a piece of machinery isn't all that uncommon, but this was a little different.

She had her hair all screwed up in curls with her ear rings and lipstick on.....didn't look like a ranch hand to me. "Just because I work like a man doesn't mean I have to look like one."

"What happens if you bust something? Won't you get all messed up tryin' to fix it?"

"I just drive it....if something breaks, ol' what's-his-face has to fix it." That's the term of endearment she sometimes uses for her dear hubby.

A few years ago this same finely coiffured lady stopped in town to pick up a lady preacher from back east to give her a ride out to a country wedding some forty miles or so in the Bear Paws. She was also giving a lift to a couple of other ladies as well as ol' Buster MacLeod.....(he's the one that told me the story.) Buster was settin' in the middle of the back seat of the neighbor lady's Lincoln between these two fine lookin' gals, with the lady preacher in the passenger seat in the front.

"...an' the rocks were flyin' over the fence posts on both sides of the road."

Bless this lady preacher's heart, she just wasn't used to country ways. I doubt if she'd ever been off of the blacktop before. This neighbor lady of ours pretty much drives with the hammer down, and the rocks were flyin' over the fence posts on both sides of the road by the time she got that old Lincoln into over drive.

The two gals in the back and the driver were having a fine conversation, but Buster said that the preacher lady was hangin' on to the dash board and sayin' some sort of religious soundin' stuff to herself.

80

They kept pickin' up speed as they went along....you can't be late to a marryin' if you're the one haulin' the preacher. No one else seemed to notice, but Buster said that the faster the car got to goin' the louder the lady preacher got to mutterin'.

They were battin' along about sixty or so, when they topped a little rise, and there was a big ol' rattler layin' there sunnin' himself in the middle of the road. It's just plain reflex for a country girl to skid on a snake, so the driver locks up all four wheels. The gravel is hittin' the bottom of the car, the preacher is gettin' real loud by now, and the snake is huntin' a hole.

Dust is completely enveloping the scene, as the neighbor lady cramps the wheel hard right and throws the car into a skid. "What in the name of the Lord are you doing?" the lady preacher shrieks.

"I'm going to make sure I got that snake," was the reply as the she finishes a nearly perfect bootlegger turn. Ol' Lead Foot is really walkin' on the gas pedal now, and the Lincoln is headed back to town through it's own dust. The normally pleasant driver now has a nearly demonic look as her focus and intentions are bull's eyed on Mr. Snake.

"When you grow up in snake country, you make dang sure they're dead," she says as she skids to a stop through what's left of the snake. "Got him! Boy, he's a big one. Do you want me to cut the rattles off for you?" she asks the lady preacher as she reaches into her purse and pulls out a six inch lock blade knife.

She never did get an answer. The lady preacher's eyes were plumb shut, and it was plain that the religious soundin' stuff was actually prayin'.

Some girls sure seem to scare easier than others.

Lyin'

Way out West in Montana, the wind don't ever blow
It's always warm and sunny, an' there's never ice or snow
The cowgirls wear bikinis, they're accoutrements to share
An' the grass is tall and blowin', in the breeze that isn't there
Where right is right, and wrong is wrong ....

                                    and a man's word's his bond
I think mine musta come unglued, I been lyin' for so long

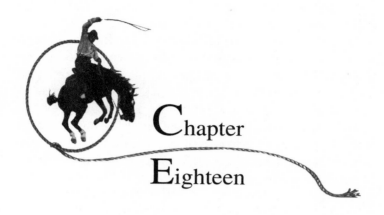

Chapter Eighteen

The Kryptonite Cowboy

When I was a kid all the little boys wanted to grow up to be cowboys... at least the smart ones. After all, cowboys were brave and handsome, and they had fancy horses and pistols and everything. They beat up bad guys and saved the pretty girl from the mean man with the mustache that wanted to get the deed to her ranch. Who in their right mind wouldn't want to be like that?

Myron, that's who. He wanted to grow up to be Superman. He always was a little strange that boy. No cowboy stuff for Myron. He was always traipsing around with his sister's beach towel around his shoulders and a big red S on his tee shirt.

There was just one little problem with his plan. The rest of us could actually grow up and be real cowboys (even if it wasn't quite as exciting as we thought), while poor ol' Myron was in a dream world. He didn't have any Kryptonite. That's what gave

Superman his great strength, you know. Kryptonite is a little hard to come by.... being fictional and all, but you'd never convince Myron of that.

He was always on the lookout for it. That's when Billy Thompson came up with the plan. He figured if we could just convince ol' Myron that this Superman idea if his was all baloney, then we could all be cowboys. After all, he really wasn't a bad guy, and he'd probably make a great addition to the gang.

Billy's Dad had a little foot rot in some of his yearlin's, and the vet had gotten him some weird lookin', greenish-yellow medicated salt to try to clear 'em up. It was the strangest lookin' stuff you ever saw. It smelled weird, too. I can't recall if the heifers got cured up or not, but I do remember Billy getting about a half a coffee can of that concoction, and comin' up with this cock and bull story to convince Myron he had some genuine Kryptonite.

He told him somethin' about a professor at the college, and about it bein' a secret. Myron swore he'd never tell a soul. Billy told him the professor said that all a feller had to do was to put a little bit of this stuff in a plastic bag and sleep with it under his pillow for a week or so. That way the power would soak right out of the Kryptonite and into your brain when you're sleepin'. Myron bought it.... hook, line, and sinker.

Billy was innocent enough.... at least his motives were pure. He knew that Superman stuff was all BS, bein' in the second grade and all, and Myron really would make a good cowboy. It was kinda fun to watch for the next few days.

Every time Myron would go past a mirror, you could see him flexing his Mighty Mouse muscles to see if they had grown any, and he was almost never seen without that durn beach towel.... I mean cape, around his shoulders. He took to hoppin' off the porch at least a hundred times a day to see if he could get airborne.

After a week or ten days of this, Myron had totally convinced himself that his muscles truly were growin', and all he needed to really fly was a little more elevation. That's when the plan went a little haywire. He did a perfect swan dive out of the loft of Anderson's barn, but just couldn't seem to get the hang of flyin'. Thank God for that manure pile. Billy would have been in big trouble if poor Ol' Myron had killed himself on his maiden flight.... especially if the Kryptonite story had gotten out.

We finally won him over. Myron gave up on that crazy Superman idea, and joined up with the rest of us. That nosedive crash landing into the manure pile was the last straw. He was going to be a real cowboy now, Mighty Mouse muscles and all. We had a great time us boys.

Sometimes I feel sad that the little boys nowadays don't have the cowboy heroes we had when we were kids. I think the good old USA started downhill when the cowboys were taken off the Saturday afternoon matinee. Right was right, wrong was wrong, and there really wasn't any in between.

There are a lot of grown up folks nowadays that are just as screwed up as Myron was when he was a kid. They're under the impression that it takes somethin' special from outer space or someplace to help you accomplish great things. You know, real heroes aren't born they're made... and it doesn't even take any Kryptonite.

They're just ordinary folks like you and me that rise above a difficult situation to do what's right... just because it's right and it needs doin'. We're really fortunate to live way out here where we do; away from all the mess in the cities. All of us wish we could do more to help. I'm not too sure we can't. Take a stand for what's right. Be a hero....just because it needs doin'.

Wood heat feels so good when the air is cold and breezy
But it's hard to beat that bottle gas....

                     ... it's so Dad-blamed easy.

Chapter

Nineteen

Tail of Two Traders

*T*radin' cattle for a living really isn't for the faint of heart. I'm of the opinion that if the government would just put a good cattle buyer in charge of our foreign trade and pay him on a commission, our troubles would be over. Better yet, use two traders and let them compete for who made the best deals. Competition is what keeps their motors runnin'. The money is really secondary.... it's just how they keep score. Most of 'em have nerves of steel and a banker with an ulcer.

There are a couple of ol' boys that I used to trade with a few years ago that really illustrate my point. Jack and Dave are both in a nursing home now, but in their day they cut a pretty wide swath in the cattle business. They've been friends for at least fifty years, but the competition between them got pretty fierce at times. In fact they're still in competition.... it's just a way of life for them.

I stop by and visit with the ol' boys on occasion to try to brighten their day a little, and they usually wind up brightenin' mine. They've always got their wheel chairs pulled over in the sun on the porch, and as they argue over a game of Pitch, they're tryin' to outdo the other guy in gaining the attention of some nurse that's at least forty years younger than they are. I forgot to tell you that cattle traders are also born optimists. They haven't stopped to think about what would happen if she took them up on one of their frequent propositions.

One day I stopped by and Jack was busy tellin' about the dream he'd had the night before.

"Man, you shoulda been there. I was in Billings at the sale barn and those Thompson steers were in town. You remember how you always used to run me up on those steers, don't you Dave? Boy, this dream was somethin'! Those steers were the best they'd ever raised.

"Lots of money... purty girls, it must be a tough way to make a livin'."

Ever' one looked just like the one before. They looked like they were cut out with a cookie cutter.... 1500 of the best son of a guns you ever saw. We'd had a little storm the night before, and the cattle were really shrunk up. You talk about a weighin' condition, they had it.... and to make things even better, the storm had kept a lot of the buyers home, there were only three or four of us there."

"Yea, yea...(Dave wasn't impressed.) Shut up and deal the cards."

Jack spit a big wad of brown lookin' goo out in the coffee can tied to the arm of his chair, and went on like he hadn't even heard him. He looked up in the air, staring off into space as he relived the moment and continued, "They had a hard time even gettin' a bid..... an' you didn't even have an order!" he smiled a broad toothless grin. "I bought the durn things ten bucks under the market, sent them down to Omaha and made a killin'!" he concluded triumphantly as he tried to goose the passing nurse.

Dave just looked at him in disgust. "You musta been dreamin'. That's the only way you'd ever get those Thompson steers away from me. Besides," he looked slyly over his glasses, "I had a dream last night, too."

"Oh yea?" says Jack, "It couldn't have been as good as mine."

Dave pretended to not even hear as he launched into the telling of a tale of his own. "I was back out at the ranch, and it was twenty years ago. Almost dark one night, there was a knock on the door. When I went to answer it, there stood the two most beautiful women I've ever seen.

It seems that their car was busted down, and here they were stranded way out in the country. I, bein' a gentleman and all, offered to see if I could get it fixed for 'em. They were all flustered.... you know how women can get, but I assured them I'd get things all straightened out. Doggone it, the way it turns out, they were a couple of Hollywood movie stars and were headed over in the mountains to make a big movin' picture. One of 'em was a long legged blond that spoke with a cute little foreign accent, and the other one was a foxy little red head.... boy, she was somethin'." He then began a detailed description of some of their finer and most interesting physical qualities.

"Then what happened? Go on....go on," Jack stammered as he fiddled with the fringe on his afghan.

Dave really had an audience now, so he continued. "It really wasn't anything serious with their car, I had it fixed in no time, and offered to show them a little western hospitality. We went back to the ranch and barbecued some steaks. You talk about a couple of friendly gals, **WHOOOEEEE**! Boy, did we have us a time!" he trailed off as he left it up to his old friend to fill in the blanks.

Jack got plumb upset. "Dad blame it, Dave, I thought we was friends! I didn't live but twenty miles from you. Why in the dickens didn't you give me a call? What in the world is a sorry ol' cow buyer like you gonna do with two gorgeous women anyway? You shoulda called me, Dave. Dang it, I'd a called you!"

Dave just looked over his glasses again, "I tried to call you Jack, honest I did….. they told me you were in Billings at the sale."

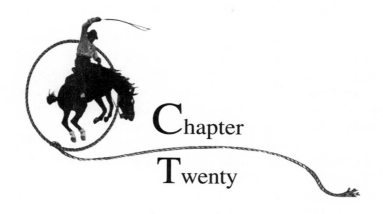

Chapter Twenty

Tradin' With Carl

Things sure have changed. When I was a kid goin' to town was a big deal... and it really wasn't all that far. Nowadays there are folks that drive 150 miles one way just to buy groceries, and drive by a dozen or so grocery stores in the process. I really used to look forward to those trips to town with my Dad or my Grandad. Anytime they would need to run into town to pick up some parts or supplies, you can bet your bottom dollar that I was sure to tag along.

One of my favorite spots to stop was at Carl's. Carl Gomavitz ran the Hi-Land Junk and Fur, and carried a lot of the essentials needed to keep our old place goin'. Carl sold all kinds of fencin' material and iron, as well as nails and wool sacks and a huge assortment of other stuff a rancher just can't get along without. He also bought scrap iron and old batteries as well as hides and furs. I remember once he was buying jackrabbits, and shipping them out to use for mink farm food. He sometimes had a truckload of dead jackrabbits out behind his building. He had a real gift for figurin' a way to make money on just about anything.

He was a tall angular built man with long arms, about the same age as my Grandad, and had emigrated from someplace in Eastern Europe. His heritage was Jewish, and although he had little if any education, he was one sharp cookie. What I liked about going to Carl's was that he was different than everyone else I knew, and I was intrigued by his thick accent, and by the way that he had taught himself to figure money. It was certainly unorthodoxed and totally backwards, but it somehow seemed to work for him. I remember specifically one instance when Dad had bought a few things, and had asked Carl what he owed him.

"That vill be a dollar and a half and fifteen nickels." That's a little hard to follow if you're not used to it, but he always seemed to come up with the right total somehow.

I wish now that I'd taken the time to get to know him a little better. He had some tales to tell that would curl your hair. Dad asked him once how he happened to come to America, and I'll never forget the story he told.

"I vuz nineteen years oldt. Der vuz some soldiers dat hadt a bunch of us in da back of a couple of oldt trucks. Dey saidt dey vuz takin' us out to verk in some farm fields. Dey spoke a different language dan us, and dey didn't know I couldt understand dem. Nobody else couldt but me. Dey stopped da trucks after a long time, and told us to get out and stretch our legs an' go to da batroom if ve needed to. Dey set up a machine gun to guardt us vit.

Den I heard da commander say, "Shoot dem like dogs." I vuz da only vun dat couldt understandt dem, and I yelled at da udders to run, and I took off as fast

92

as I couldt go. Dat machine gun started shootin' and der vuz lots of yellin', but I never looked back, and I never quit runnin' 'til I got here."

Being raised in the sheltered environment of the rural west, my ten year old eye balls must have been the size of a couple of silver dollars. This was the first time I'd ever heard a first hand account of somethin' that sounded like it had come out of some war movie. Unfortunately that wasn't the end of the story.

Carl went on, "My brother vuz on dat truck vit me, an' I never saw him again. I don't know if he made it or not. If he did, I don't know vut ever happened to him. I never saw none of da udders after dat..... I just kept runnin' 'til I couldn't run no more." Every time I think about that story of Carl's, I thank the Good Lord for growing up where I did.

He was certainly a shrewd man to deal with, and you had to get up before breakfast if you wanted to get ahead of him. He said that he worked on a one percent markup.

"I buy it for vun dollar and sell it for two. Dat's vun percent."

Of course, I s'pose tryin' to make a livin' on old batteries and dead jackrabbits could tend to make a feller a little on the shrewd side. One fall we had butchered a beef and Dad hauled the hide in to sell it to Carl. He had it all folded up and tied with a piece of twine, and Carl drug it over to the scales. He was buying it by the pound, and soon announced that he'd have to dock us twenty-five cents because "da earss are still on da hide". Dad just agreed, and took the dock without any complaint.

We got back in the pickup and started for home, and I just couldn't help askin', "Wasn't twenty five cents way too much to dock for just two ears? They couldn't have weighed that much."

"Yup, it was *way* too much," grinned Dad, "but I knew he was goin' to dock us for somethin'.... that's why I left the bone in the tail. We're about even."

Teddy Powell in the '60s

Owner, Manager & Fourth in Command
At the TP Bar

Chapter Twenty-One

The Real Test of a Cowboy

The little woman just insulted my hat. Boy, I hate that. So I looked in the mirror, and by George I think she's right. It really doesn't look all that good. Now, this wasn't my town hat....just for the record. This is the ol' work one, but it just may be time to put her out to pasture.

We've been through a lot together, that old hat and me. It's hard to tell just how many times it's been stomped in the manure, most of the time with my head still in it. I sure hope I don't look as rough as it does. It's really too bad that hats don't heal back up like heads do.

In this modern world full of drugstore cowboys, real ones are gettin' a little harder to come by. You know, one of the ways you can tell a real cowboy is by his hat. Oh, they certainly don't all look the same that's for sure, it has a lot more to do with the way they wear 'em.

You'll very rarely see a real cowboy chasin' his hat. I don't care if there's a forty mile an hour Chinook wind blowing, his old sky piece will be right where she belongs. The secret here is to pull it down over the knot. Every real cowboy has at least one or two knots on their head, which is why the hats get to lookin' a little rough after while. There are several on mine, but I feel very fortunate that there ain't no evidence of drain bramage.

My favorite knot for keepin' my hat on is sort of on the south west corner of my head. I got it a long time ago at a rodeo, and it still sticks out good enough to keep a hat right where she belongs.

Tan lines are another good way to tell a real cowboy. A real hand's tan line will start about an inch above his eyebrows and end around three inches south of his chin. Other than his hands, the rest of him looks sort of like the belly on a fish. I saw one ol' boy get talked into gettin' into a pair of Bermuda shorts. I'll tell you what, those skinny little bowlegs were sight for sore eyes.

Someone hollered at him, "Are those really yer legs, or are you standin' on a chicken?"

I just found out something that will take a little more checkin' out, but if it holds true with a little more measuring, we finally may have a sure fire way to tell a real cowboy. I know a real good hand that had the misfortune of being the guest of honor at a wreck involving a horse and a cow last spring, and he bunged up one shoulder so bad he couldn't use it. His ol' lady finally talked him into goin' to the doctor after a week or so of laying in the corral moanin', and the Doc tied it down to his side, and told him not to use it. That didn't make a whole lot of sense to me, 'cause he couldn't move it anyway, but that's when we found out what makes cowboys different.

With one arm plumb out of commission, this ol' boy was forced to do ever'thing with his left hand. There

"Dang it! It wasn't funny!
You just try 'er with the wrong hand!"

was one particular personal chore he had to attend to ever' mornin' at 5:30 AM rain or shine. He just couldn't get it done left-handed. He just plain couldn't reach where he needed to reach. It was awful.

I saw him on the road one day, and suggested that it was probably because his left arm was four or five inches shorter than his right one, as that was about how much his reach was short. That seemed to make a lot of sense, but after measuring his arms, they were exactly the same. That's when we came to the only other obvious conclusion. He must have been bored off center.

Oh no... I didn't have anything to do with any more measurin', but I tried the same maneuver as he did, and got the same results. I measured my arms too.....same length. I think maybe it must be a universal problem unique to cowboys.

Now I've known some guys I thought were bored a little oversize, but I've never even thought about off center. I'll be doggoned. I ain't tellin' who this ol' boy is, but his brand is TP Bar.

Chapter Twenty-Two

The Secret Identity

It was a warm spring mornin' with the sun just peeking over the eastern hills, but already Pookey was circling his pen with the cheers of the Las Vegas rodeo crowd in his ears. Although he was really still in his little bucket calf pen near the Milk River in Montana, Pookey had dreams of one day being a famous bucking bull. In fact, he was pretending to be the most famous bull of them all....the mighty Bodacious.

He practiced his moves constantly, and watched his shadow as his bucks and spins improved daily. He also was practicing letting his ears hang down low. Every one knows that a mighty buckin' bull had to have at least a little Brahman blood in his veins. He worked hard and long at looking ferocious, and imagined he had long horns and a big hump on his shoulders. The fact that he was just a 500 pound Hereford bucket calf, with a life changing operation in his future didn't seem to dampen his spirits a bit. Calves have an imagination too, you know.

After one especially strenuous early morning of bucks and spins, Pookey was resting in the middle of the pen, trying to catch his breath and practicing holding his ears down low....just like Bodacious. He glanced up to see his Ma coming down the path from the house. Oh, it wasn't his real Ma... he'd never known her. Peggy was his adopted Ma, and took great care of him and the other orphans in the pen. In fact, she probably loved him more than his real mother had.

"Oh, I wish I could tell her about my dream to be the greatest buckin' bull of all time," thought Pookey to himself, but as hard as he tried, she just didn't seem to understand.

"Pookey! Baby!" shrieked his feisty little red headed adopted Mom. "Your ears are hanging down and you look exhausted. You must be sick, you poor baby. Just wait right here, Mama will get something to make you all better."

"Sick my foot!" thought Pookey, "A buckin' bulls ears are 'sposed to look like this."

It was too late. Peggy was already halfway back to the house. She got on the phone to her buddy Lorraine who ran a feedlot and was up on all the latest sick calf treatments. Help was now on the way and within the hour, the two lady cowboys were stepping into the bucket calf pen armed with a vast assortment of needles, pills, and what appeared to Pookey to be instruments of shear torture.

"Should we run him into the chute?" asks Peggy's blonde helper.

"Naw. Pookey's really gentle. I can just hold him," was the answer as the redhead straddled her baby's neck and lifted up his chin to receive a couple of pills.

"You're not sittin' on Pookey," thought the calf to himself, "I am the mighty Bodacious, the most famous buckin' bull of all time. You're just lucky that you're my Ma....that's all. I wonder where she dug up that sissy Pookey name, anyway? "

He suffered through the bolus gun and those awful tasting sulfa pills and even the pain of the two injections, but when Lorraine twisted his tail out of the way to take his temperature, it was just more than he could take. You just won't believe where she put that thermometer. It was simply more indignity than a mighty rodeo bull of his stature should have to endure. Bodacious came uncorked.

Peggy is a heck of a hand, but she just wasn't any match for the greatest buckin' bull of all time. Although there wasn't a timer available, it's very doubtful she made the whistle. Peggy wanted to cry, and Lorraine could hardly standup from laughing so hard.

"I hate to tell you lady, but I don't think you made the whistle....but if you did, you only marked a 24."

Pookey was triumphant. All of his practice had paid off in Spades. For a withering eight seconds...... he **WAS** Bodacious.

Chapter Twenty-Three

Just Tired of Walkin'

I ran into John Faber not too long ago. He grew up out in the Bear Paws, and so he and I rode on different circles growin' up. I really didn't get to know him very well until he bought an outfit down on the river. That must have been sometime in the '60s.

Back before all these new fangled "pour on treatments" for cattle came out, everyone in the neighborhood used to run their cows through the dippin' vat down at his place in the fall. He's somehow gotten himself hired as the manager of the Montana State Prison Ranch down at Deer Lodge now, and whatever they're payin' him, they're getting a good deal. He's a heck of a hand.

That's the main reason I should've smelled a rat when he asked me to ride one of his horses for a few days. Although it turned out all right, he told me it was because he was just too busy. (Yea, right.) It was back in the 70's sometime when I got the call.

"Come on down in the mornin'. Herman is comin' over to cut 'im. He's still a stud."

Herman Friede was a good old boy, and the man to call if you needed to geld a colt. That's probably how I got the ridin' job. I used to follow him around trying to learn the finer points of his technique. He was the master of a nearly lost art. I can't remember ever seeing him when he had any teeth.

A barrel chested bull of a man with a wide toothless grin, he quite frankly didn't look like your stereotypical cowboy, but he dang shore knew how to throw a horse and get the job done. He'd taken a likin' to me, and was really showing me the ropes. We both wound up at John's about the same time one morning, and our victim.... I mean patient, was already locked in the round corral. He was a big stout heavy boned four year old buckskin.

"He ain't halter broke.... we'll have to front foot him."

We got the job done with John and I doing the bonehead chores and Herman directin' traffic, and decided it would be best to turn him back out to heal up for a few days before I took him home.

A couple of weeks later I went back down to pick up my spring project. To say Ol'Buck wasn't happy to see us would be an understatement. He rolled a big white eyeball at us and gave us a snort, as if to say, "Oh no! Not these guys again!" The only other contact he'd had with human bein's was us, and the way he figured it, the last deal hadn't turned out all that well.

We had to front foot him again to get the halter on, and then tied him up to the corral to pout awhile while we had a cup of coffee. After a few minutes he'd settled down and nearly quit fightin' the lead rope, so it was time to try to get some wheels under him.

It sure looked like the safest to bring the trailer into the corral. There just wasn't any way we could hold the big bugger if he took his head and decided to run. John had a little short two horse trailer with a big bump in the floor where the axle went through. It was long enough for the horse, but there dang shore wasn't any extra room. We had a real rodeo on our hands when Ol' Buck figured out he wasn't tied to the post anymore, but we had a long chunk of rope on him, so the two of us managed to hold him alright. We finally got him snubbed up to the ring in the front of the trailer, and kept urging him forward and takin' up the slack a little at a time.

"Take it easy with him. We don't want to tangle up his thinkin' any worse than it already is."

We got the front end of that cayuse loaded, but his chin was snubbed up tight against the cinch ring in the trailer, and we had over half of him stickin' out the back. We were havin' a dickens of a time, and tried everything we could think of, but Ol' Buck wasn't budgin' one more inch. We tried the rope under the tail trick.... nope. We even tried a little persuasion with the knot in the end of the lariat.... that didn't work either.

After an hour or so John says, "You get a hold of the trailer door, and when he gets in, you shut it."

"Good idea," I thinks to myself, "I think I can handle that." There didn't seem to be much danger of that happening anytime soon.

John swung the corral gate open wide and climbed in his old pickup. He started it up, stuck 'er in compound low and idled out into the ranch yard. Ol' Buck's front end was ridin', and his backend was standin'. Somethin' had to change. He'd never been tied to anything that moved before. He did the usual "pull back and get away from this contraption" routine about twice, then stepped right into the trailer. I slammed the door, and John came to the back with a big wide grin on his face.

"It's an old Indian trick. I thought he'd get tired of walkin' after while." ⸻≪≫⸻

Ode to the Lonely Biffy

Under these spreading Cottonwoods
I've stood the test of time
Every size and shape of derriere
Has graced this seat of pine

I knew that time was runnin' out
And I could see the day a comin'
When they'd no longer tread my path
....That Dad-blamed indoor plumbin'

Then one mornin' at forty below
Once more my throne they chose
An indoor pot ain't much good
When all the pipes is froze

106

Chapter Twenty-Four

Uncle Eugene and the Snake

I know everybody has seen that little sign outside of eatin' places and stores that says, "No shirt, no shoes, no service." Most folks think that probably the health department had somethin' to do with it, or maybe it was The National Society for the Proliferation of Tee Shirts and Sneakers. Now, both of those groups would have a real interest in seein' that folks was properly covered up, but in reality, it wasn't either one of 'em.

Nope. It all started many years ago in a little town called Goosegrease, Montana. Actually, Goosegrease wasn't even a town until my Uncle Eugene got there, and then it really got started just by accident.

Uncle Eugene was a freighter, and had a contract to haul supplies from Fort Benton on the Missouri river north to Fort MacLeod in what is now

Alberta. Fort Benton was as far up the Missouri as the old stern wheelers could go, and was a real hub of commerce in the late 1800s.

It was a real dry summer in 1874 or '75, and with the water level bein' so low, the freight was slow comin' up river, so Uncle Eugene took a job haulin' lumber from a mill on the south side of the Bear Paw Mountains to the little settlement of Carlisle up by the Canadian border. It was towards the end of July and he had two big freight wagons hooked together piled as full as he could get 'em with Bear Paw fir lumber, with ten of his best mules hitched to the outfit.

The first couple of days things went fine, but he ran into trouble in a big coulee just south of the Milk River ford. Just as they topped a little rise, they ran onto the biggest rattlesnake he'd ever seen... right in the middle of the trail. With that many mules in the hitch, and with the hump in the road, three of the teams had already passed the ol' viper before Uncle Eugene even saw it. At least half of 'em musta given him a little stomp as they passed, because his temper was gettin' plumb out of control and that ol' snake was a bitin' at everything that went by.

He was a big one, too... at least six or seven feet long and as big as a man's leg. The mules were all purty snake savvy, and avoided gettin' bit, which must be awful frustratin' if yer a snake. The only thing that didn't duck 'er dodge was the wagon tongue, so when it got within strikin' range that ol' snake really sunk his teeth into it.

Uncle Eugene was a fast thinker... you had to be in those days. In one smooth move, he set the brake on the wagon, pulled the hitch pin to let the mules go, and reached under the seat for his axe. That ol' snake was latched onto that wagon tongue like a bull dog on a mailman... bittin' like his life depended on it. I guess it did, fer if he'd a turned loose he might have avoided a very painful death. Uncle Eugene dispatched Mr.

Snake with a half a dozen well placed blows between the eyes, and then set to cuttin' the tongue out of the wagon as fast as he could. It was too late. The venom had already soaked up the tongue and into the wagon. It was a goner.

What in the world do you do out in the middle of no place with two dead wagons full of fir lumber? I think Uncle Eugene musta been a genius. He tore them wagons apart right there and built the Dead Wagon Saloon and General Store with the lumber. Bein' right near the river and on the trail to Carlisle, he soon had a good business, other folks began to settle there, and before you know it, Goosegrease was on the map. It became a regular stoppin' place for all sorts of pilgrims, and business was boomin'.

"A snake that size must have at least a gallon or two o' poison."

'Course it never became public knowledge as to how the saloon got it's name. It might be bad for business. Venom soaked lumber might just scare off a tenderfoot with money to spend, even though it was plumb safe... except on rare occasions.

The only time there was a problem was when it was real hot. A snake that size has probably got a gallon or two of poison, and the heat seemed to make it come a soakin' out of the boards. If a feller was bare footed or leaned up again' the wall with his shirt off, it could prove to be fatal. It fact, that very thing happened a time or two, which led Uncle Eugene to put up the sign; "No shirt, no shoes, no service".

His business was so good that merchants for miles around thought that little sign must be the key to his success, so they all copied him. As a matter of fact, they're still doin' it today, and not a one of 'em knows the real reason why.

109

"Now **THAT** was ridiculous."

Chapter Twenty-Five

Victoria's Secret

$\mathcal{B}$arry and Victoria run some yearlin's and raise a little corn and wheat in western Kansas. "Bear" is the fourth generation of his family to work the place. He also travels quite a bit singin' cowboy songs and doing his poetry.... he's pretty dang good at it, too. They are just good ol' "salt of the earth" kind of people. We've bumped into them several times through the years, and have gotten to know them pretty well.

Bear's Dad is semi-retired and has moved into town, but I think the deal is sort of like my Dad, he still stays pretty busy out on the place. Bear probably gets about as much free labor out of his ol' Dad as I do mine.

In fact it is said that in western Kansas a lot of folks set their watch by the time that his "retired" Dad heads out from town to go to work. Every morning at 7:30 that silver Dodge pickup can be seen coming down the road....just like clock work. You can count on it.

Victoria is Bear's better half. What a peach of a gal. Although she has been a good ranch wife, and helps out on the place all the time just doin' what needs to be done, she quite frankly isn't just your typical ranch lady. She looks like she should have been a model instead of a cowgirl. In fact, in my opinion, she makes Miss America look sorta like chopped liver.

"That's the best lookin' gal in Kansas," I heard one ol' boy say.

Although I don't think I've had the opportunity to meet all the ladies from down that way.... yet, I've got a tendency to think the old guy knew what he was talkin' about. I really believe him. She's just as pretty on the inside as she is on the outside too, but it's the way the outside of her looks that has caused a major shift in the traffic patterns in western Kansas. Let me explain.

An awful lot of that part of the country is pretty flat, and their area is no exception. You can see forever. I think you could see the back of your own head if your eyes were good enough. One mornin' just about 7:30 as Victoria was headed out to the mailbox, she looked up and sure enough just like clock work, here came that familiar silver Dodge pickup down the road from town.

It was fastly approaching as she finished placing the letters in the box, so being in the mood to be a little silly, she lifted her long denim prairie skirt above her knee, flashed her most seductive smile, and stuck up her thumb. The pickup roared on past, although the driving did seem a little erratic. "I sure got ol' Dad," she laughed to herself as she skipped back to the house, "I wonder why he didn't turn in?"

Bear was witness to the entire escapade, and inquired of his lovely bride, "What was that all about?"

"I just thought I'd have some fun with your Dad," she giggled, "where's he going anyway?"

"That wasn't Dad," was the reply as Dad's silver Dodge pickup pulled into the yard, "that was the Thompson kid that works in town at the tire shop."

Victoria was mortified. Although her flushing cheeks have since regained most of their original color, it's doubtful that things will be back to normal in those parts for some time to come. After the story got around in that sleepy little rural community, it appears for some strange reason, that they've experienced a sizable increase in traffic past their mailbox every morning about 7:30.

That seems perfectly reasonable to me. If it just wasn't so doggone far to Kansas, I'd swing by there ever' morning myself.

The Wild Bunch

Standing, L to R:
Will Carver (alias Cowboy Bill)
Harvey Logan (alias Kid Curry)
Sitting :
Harry Longabaugh (alias The Sundance Kid)
Ben Kilpatrick (alias The Tall Texan)
Robert Leroy Parker (alias Butch Cassidy)

(Photo stolen from The Wild Bunch)

Chapter Twenty-Six

More 'n One Way to Skin a Cat

Granny used to say, "There's more 'n one way to skin a cat". I just heard a story that was told to a friend of mine by an old timer that rode with the "Wild Bunch" or the "Hole in the Wall Gang", as they were sometimes called, (the members sort of floated back and forth) and it brought that old sayin' back to mind.

Because of the movie, probably most everyone's heard of the most famous members, Butch Cassidy and the Sundance Kid. They had quite a gang at one time, which included our local desperado Kid Curry. Among the antics of various members was the Great Northern train robbery near Wagner, Montana in 1901. Butch and Sundance were already in South America by then, and the ring leader on that deal was the Kid. Grandpa Olson ran into Kid Curry once in a saloon in what was to become Lohman, Montana. He said he didn't know who he was, but that he was at the end of the bar alone. He remembered he looked mean, and was packin' a pearl handled pistol. "I didn't like da look in his eye. I knew he vuzn't yust a cowpuncher." After he left, Grandpa asked someone who he was.

"That's Kid Curry. Leave him alone."

The old timer relating this story was a "horse holder", as opposed to one of the actual gunmen. The gang's plan of action was to have fresh horses held at secret locations, and placed about a day's ride apart. The logic was fairly simple. If the posse had tired horses, and yours were fresh, gettin' away was a cinch. The "Hole in the Wall" was the name of their hideout in Wyoming. It really only had one way in, so watchin' the door was fairly easy.

Robbin' banks in Wyoming and Montana at the turn of the century wasn't all that lucrative, as there wasn't any money in 'em. If the poor old ranchers happened to make a few bucks, they didn't dare put it in the bank for fear that the banker would think it was a payment on their past due notes. The only way to hang on to it was to bury it.

Now, Utah was a different story. The banks there were plum full of cash, and everyone put their money in the bank....which leads to the bitter-sweet problem. When you robbed a bank in Utah, everyone in the county chased you out of town trying to get their money back. That's where the fresh horses came in mighty handy. The gang would station holders with fresh horses all the way back to Wyoming. They'd hole up in the canyons during the day, and push 'em down to the meadows to graze at night.

Problem was, they just didn't have enough holders, so when they were a few days away from the lucky bank that had been the recipient of their famous "early withdrawal" plan, they would make a deal with a hard scrabble rancher to pasture some horses for 'em, with the agreement he would have them in the corral on a certain day. The ranchers didn't ask any questions, and were plum happy to make a few extra dollars.

On one occasion they showed up at this little Wyoming ranch, and sure enough, the horses were in the corral, right on schedule. The old rancher said, "It's sure a good thing you boys got here today instead of tomorrow. The banker called our loan, and is comin' out this afternoon for his money. We ain't got a prayer of payin' him off. He'll be takin' over, and we'll be out of here by tonight." The situation was really desperate.

"Man, oh man," said the Hole in the Wall Boys. "That's too bad. You folks have worked so hard here, too. All you need is a chance, and you'll make it. How much money do you owe him?" The figure was $3000.00, quite a tidy chunk of change for the times, but it just so happened, the visitors had a little cash on 'em.

"Here ya go. You've been good to us, and always pastured our stock when we needed it. If anyone ever deserved a helpin' hand, you folks do. When that banker comes out, you just pay him off. But what ever you do, don't forget to get a receipt. You know how them bankers are. Ever'body knows you can't trust 'em."

The poor old ranch family couldn't believe their good fortune. They had both fists full of cash, and shore enough, the banker showed up after dinner, right on schedule. Boy, you should have seen the look on his face when they forked over the cash 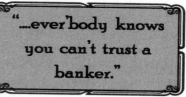 and paid him in full. He had no idea they had that kind of money, and was plum relieved. The last thing he wanted was another ranch. He wrote their receipt and headed back to town.

The ranch was quite a ways back in the hills, and about half way to town, as the banker stopped his buggy to water and rest his horse at a little stream, he was greeted by a gang of armed men. News reports say that; "The men just seemed to know I had money."

All those modern financial wizards just think they invented creative financin'. The old horse holder wouldn't divulge the name of the ranch. "'Cause their grand kids still run the place, and I ain't sure how they'd take it."

Just remember when it comes to handlin' a difficult problem, it's just like Granny said, "There's more 'n one way to skin a cat."

Chapter Twenty-Seven

My Little Poodle-Pit Bull Cross

I never get to buy anyone anything for Christmas. By the time I get in the spirit of things, the little woman has been done shoppin' for a couple of months. There is only one time I can think of where I finally got my turn. It was while we were in Tucson for the Western Music Association Festival a few years ago, and had taken a side trip to one of those little border towns in Mexico. Now that was an experience. 'Course we'd been there once before, but just in case you haven't, get prepared for culture shock. It's a real horse trader's heaven. If you pay the first price asked, you've just been slickerd.

Now my little cook isn't much of a trader. She just hates it when I get to chiselin' to get a little better deal. But, now to her credit, she's mighty tight with a dollar, she just claims not to be a trader. Well, it so happens she found this perfect gift. "That would be great to give Uncle Harry. She only wants 20 bucks for it, but I'm sure you could get it for less than that. Go deal with her."

Now I feel it's my responsibility to help her along in life, so I refused. The logic here is that I may not always be around to help out, so she needs to learn to make her own deals. The conversation went something like this.

Says I, "If you want it, buy it. I'm not going to do your tradin' for you."

She was a little miffed, but went back to the sales lady and said. "I don't deal. What did you say you wanted for that thingamajig?"

In rather broken English the lady said, "Because you are my frien'.... I sell it to you for fifteen dollors." Now that really perked the old girl up.

She came running back to me with the great news, "She said she'd take fifteen dollars."

My callused reply was the same. "If you want it buy it."

I need to mention here, just to get things in perspective, that my little wife is a Swedish/Jewish cross. Now that's a lot like crossin' a toy poodle and a pit bull, and at this point in the negotiations, her repressed pit bull tendencies were beginnin' to take control. After just the proper amount of stallin', she goes back to her new frien' and says, "I told you I don't deal. How much did you say you wanted?"

Of course, our south of the border entrepreneur can almost taste the sale now. "I tol' you that you were my frien'..... for you twelve dollors."

The reply? "I told you I don't deal. I'll give you ten."

Now this little story has a moral. If you happen by the Overcast Ranch, and are lookin' to make a deal. I suggest you don't try to match wits with my little pit bull. Of course she ain't no trader, and really hates to make deals.... it's just that she's so durn good at it. It'd be way cheaper to deal with me.

120

Chapter Twenty-Eight

Dick and Billy's Kitty Deal

This ranching deal has never been all that easy, and it doesn't look like it's going to change all that much.... at least for the better. A feller has to be thinkin' all the time just to stay in the game. There are all sorts of ingenious things that I've seen folks do to bring in a few extra bucks. A lot of them I even tried myself.

As a matter of fact, I've got this deal goin' now where I get paid to sing and play my guitar. If anyone ever lets the cat out of the bag that I really can't do either one, I'll be in big trouble. Speakin' of a cat in a bag and big trouble....... that reminds me of a story.

It happened to Dick and Billy. They're partners on this hard pan alkali outfit that would make gents of lesser constitution just plain give up.... but not those two. No-sir-ee. They're into all natural food, you know; beef steak and fermented barley. They ain't really all that particular exactly whose beef steak. It just has to be good. As far as the barley is concerned, the quality isn't as much a concern as the quantity.

Like most everyone else in the ranching business, they were having a great deal of cash flow, but it all seemed to flow down hill and away from their place.

"We've gotta think of somethin' to bring in a few extra dollars," says Dick to Billy one morning about daylight as they enjoyed their usual fare of bottled barley sandwiches. "The Breakfast of Champions" they liked to call it.

"Yup," says Billy.

Dick went on. "We dang shore need the money, with the ridin' jobs as slim as they are."

"Yup," hiccupped Billy. Dick was sort of used to Billy not saying too much while he was having breakfast, so he just went on.

"...and ever' since the E Bar Y sold out, the maverickin' has been purty slim, too."

"Yup."

"I've been doin' some thinkin'."

"Yup?"

"Yea. This is a great idea that nobody has even thought of. We can go into the Tom cat neuterin' business."

"I think you're gone nuts," belched Billy, "besides we don't know nothin' about Tom cats."

"Sure we do. I've worked on a couple of 'em, and there ain't nothin' to it. Those old ladies up town pay the Vet a fortune to take care of their babies. We can do it for half price and still make a killin'. Man, we'll really clean up."

A few days later Dick had a chance to put his plan into practice. He got wind that Mrs. Sullivan from down the road was planning on taking Tommy to the vet for a mind alterin' operation, and he decided to cut himself in on the action. (no pun intended) Bein's the Sullivan's were big dry farmers with a ton of CRP, he was sure they must have a lot of money, so he offered her the "Deluxe Plan" that included an overnight stay in their modern state of the art facility.

"What state of the art facility?" burped Billy.

"Shut up, Billy…. I'll do the talkin'."

"As I was sayin', Mrs. Sullivan, we'll take perfect care of Tommy, and deliver him back here tomorrow all refreshed with the operation only a faint memory in his little feline mind."

"What's feline mean?"

"Shut up, Billy."

They were soon rattlin' back down the road in their old pickup with Tommy in his rhinestone studded kitty cage between them on the seat. "This'll be the easiest fifty bucks we ever made," says Dick as they make the turn onto the rutted gumbo trail to the ranch.

"I still ain't sure this is a good idea. I ain't never gelded a cat in my life," slurred Billy as he opened another barley sandwich.

"It's a piece o' cake," answered Dick as they pulled up in front of the old chicken coop. "Just as well get started. Take off one of yer boots." Billy reluctantly pulled off a boot, really not too sure about what was going to happen next.

"Now when I stuff Tommy's head in yer boot, you hold the top of it together between yer knees and hang on to his back legs. I'll do the operatin'."

Billy was seated on the old choppin' block in front of the chicken coop where so many roosters had made their first stop on the trail to Granny's dumpling pan, with Tommy stuck head first into one of his boots. He had the top of the boot and Tommy's tummy held securely between his knees and a hind leg in each hand as Doctor Dick began the operation. To say that Tommy wasn't very impressed with the turn of events would be an understatement. He stuck his claws out about four inches and jerked loose from Billy's half inebriated grip. If he could have only gotten them on the ground, those legs would have been carrying him at least fifty miles an hour, but in lieu of real estate, they started cuttin' a couple of deep tracks in Billy's belly.

Tommy was squallin', and Billy was squallin', and Dick was just standing there helpless, lookin' two eyed. The cat finally jerked loose and hit the ground, throwing gravel all over the side of the chicken coop. Billy looked like he'd been in a wrestling match with a buzz saw. Man, was he ever a mess! All that was left of his denim shirt was the collar and the cuffs, and within a few seconds, Tommy was just a little calico spot on the horizon; makin' forty foot strides through the Sullivan's CRP.

"Dang it, Billy. I told you to hang on to him. There goes our fifty bucks."

"Yup," hiccupped his partner with his bleary eyes fixed upon his claw shredded stomach, "Maybe next time I'll try the operatin', and you can do the holdin'."

"Now, that's a heck of a way to make a livin'."

Chapter Twenty-Nine

To Bill or Not to Bill
(that is the question)

Sometimes you just can't win. You know, there's times when a feller tries as hard as he can, and the results still look like they came out of that big green pile behind the barn. Let me give you of an example that happened on our place some time back.

It was along in August several years ago. We had bought some land a few years previous with a dairy barn on it. It had been shut down for a while, and we had no intentions of changing that. We were interested in the hay land......not the milk cows. I was out behind the the that old barn one day and a guy drives in the yard, says he's a dairy man, and would like to rent a place to milk his cows. If you're the least bit familiar with a dairy barn, then you already know they ain't much good for anything else. I thought it was a great idea.

Things went along fine for quite some time. The check was rollin' in once a month, and I was happier

Dr. Roger Baxter & Buster
(Buster's on the left)
Veterinarian, Friend, & Champion
of drowning bucket calves everywhere

than a hog in a manure pile. Now, I still don't know what happened for sure, but after a while the ol' boy decides he's had enough of the dairy business, and tells me he's gonna sell out. Due to a severe mental deficiency I've had since birth, I buy his cows, and now am a dairyman myself. If you ever consider that please call me for some advice, and stay on the phone long enough we can get the call traced. We'll send that nice man with the white coat over. You know, the one with that little truck with the red blinky light on the top?

We couldn't find any help, we couldn't sell the cows, and the freight train wouldn't slow down enough for me to jump on. We're stuck. I was playin' in a dance band a couple nights a week, so on the weekends, I got home just in time to take off my pickin' hat and put on my milkin' hat. It ain't a good way to die, it's sort of painful, but I'm sure it'll work if you give it a little time. Between hayin' and milkin' and playin' music, the seat of my pants was startin' to drag my tracks out.

It was about dark one evenin' on a Monday. My spring was about sprung, and I'm finally headed for the rack. We did have a couple of cows that we needed to AI, but the Vet was doing that, and the little woman volunteered to show him which cows they were. He wasn't due until about 10:30. I hit the bed and died. Plumb out of gas. My dear little spouse shakes me awake about 10 minutes later with the good news that the dairy replacement heifers have rubbed the gate open, and there are four or five of them stuck in the creek. "I'm afraid they're going to drown."

My compassionate reply? "Let the #*!#*@ dumb things drown then. I'll take care of the live ones in the mornin'." There ain't nothin' dumber than a bucket calf, and these were 800 pounds of shear stupidity.

To make a long story a little shorter, after the dear ol' Vet finishes his AI chores, he volunteers to help the little woman and a neighbor lady that she'd commandeered, fish those critters out of the creek.

They had to tromp the whole end out of a cornfield to do it. It took a blue heeler, a winch truck, a Vet, sixty foot of rope, a flashlight with wore out batteries, a cattle prod, and two women about five hours in the middle of the night to get the job done. All of which, with the single exception of the winch truck, were completely submerged several times. The whole time yours truly is in never, never land with visions of sugarplums dancin' in my head.

You'd think a feller would be appreciative, wouldn't you? But the Vet has been a friend for a long time, so I just couldn't wait to run into him. About a week later, I saw him for the first time since the drownin' heifer incident. It was in a local waterin' hole in front of a whole gang of cowboys.

I says, "Doc, about the other night. I didn't ask you to help all those hours fishin' them heifers out of the creek. I just asked you to AI the two cows. I can just imagine how much that bill must be the way you Vets charge, and if you send me a bill for all that time, you an' me are gonna have troubles."

He was sort of lookin' at me two eyed, like he was tryin' to think of somethin' to say when I went on, "But after spendin' all night long with my wife in that corn patch, you dang shore **BETTER** send one!"

Sometimes a feller just can't win.

Chapter Thirty

Way Too Broke

*T*here's a sure fire way to tell when your negative cash flow has gotten out of hand. The neighbor kids even know it. We've had the opportunity to go broke a couple of times in this ranchin' business, and have so far managed to keep a stiff upper lip and "hang in there", but there was one time I couldn't even fool the neighbor kid.... and he was only six years old.

The mortgage company had foreclosed, we didn't have a dime, and were in the process of preparin' to move out of the old ranch house we thought we'd owned for ten years. I was down in the basement taking out a wood furnace we'd added on to the propane one that was there when we bought the place, when Kody the six-year-old neighborhood genius shows up to help. "Help" isn't exactly a good choice of words.... "in the way" would probably be a more appropriate term. One thing I do have to say about the little knucklehead.... he was dang shore entertaining.

"So you're movin' out, huh?"

"Yup."

"How long have you lived here anyway?" asked the little pest as he was putting some of the furnace screws in his pocket.

"Ten years."

"Holy cow! You mean you've lived here a whole century?"

Kody was a sharp little buzzard, and his folks were always reading him things out of the encyclopedia, but he must have gotten a little tangled up on that one.

"Nope, Kody," I answered as patiently as I could, not wanting to crush his inquisitive little mind. "Ten years is just a decade. A century is a hundred years." Probably because I was always teasin' him about something, he didn't believe me.

"Ho! Ho! You can't fool me! I just read it in my book this morning. Ten years is a century, and a hundred years is a decade," he retorted emphatically, slipping a pair of my pliers in his hind pocket. I think he must have been the inspirational poster child for the Dennis the Menace cartoon series.

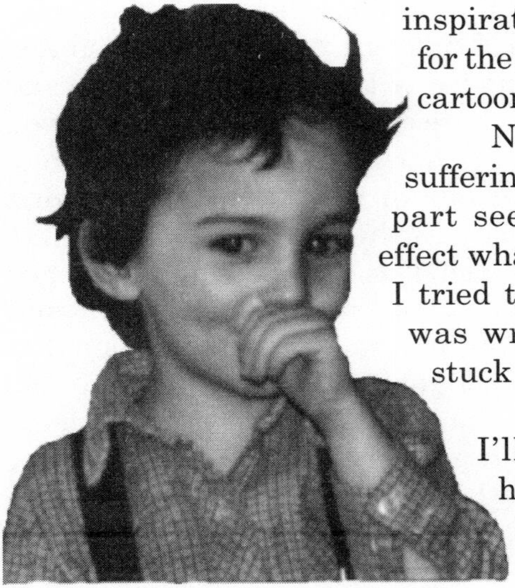

No amount of long-suffering instruction on my part seemed to have any effect whatsoever. The more I tried to convince him he was wrong, the more he stuck to his guns.

"You want to bet? I'll betcha! I'll go home and get my book and read it to you myself!" A feller could wait a lifetime for another chance at lead pipe cinch bet like this one.

"How much you want to bet, Kody?" I asked him slyly, as I was tryin' to find the proper balance between winning a bet and not takin' advantage of a little kid.

"Oh, I don't care!" answered the little nuisance, full of confidence, "I'll betcha anything you want!"

"OK," I said looking him straight in the eye. Matching his little six-year-old speech impediment the best I could, I made my proposal. "I'll bet you a fouzand dollars."

He never missed a lick. He knew I was broke, and losin' the bet was completely out of the question. After all..... he'd just read it in his book that morning. His only challenge was to be certain he made a wager he could collect.

"Ho! Ho! Oh no you don't! You can't fool me! Where are **YOU** gonna get a fouzand dollars?"

"I shore hope this next one is better than the last one."

Chapter Thirty-One

Sellin' on the Street

$\mathcal{S}$ome girls just don't have a sense of humor. The little woman that lives at our house usually does, but there are times when I can tell I've pushed her just about as close to the edge as I dare. Normally she's game for just about anything, but she drew the line on me when it came to pedalin' watermelons. She stuck it out for a couple of days....then just flat quit. Like a balkin' mule, there wasn't any use in me even wastin' my energy, because she wasn't budgin'.

I had found myself in Oklahoma in the late summer several years ago with a new pickup and a new sixteen foot stock trailer, and bein' the enterprising sort that I am, figured I needed something to haul back. Now what could I buy down south to haul back up here that would make a buck? Even when gas was thirty cents a gallon, thirty cents was hard for a country boy to find, and I was sure there must be some way to buy the gas home. I checked out the newspaper ads, but couldn't seem to find a deal on anything.

Then came a bolt of lightnin' from somewhere under my hat. **Watermelons!** We'd tried to raise 'em in the garden a few times, but they'd only gotten about the size of a grapefruit. They should sell like hot cakes up north. I located an Okie with a watermelon patch....which was about as hard as findin' a cowboy with a pair of spurs...and soon struck up a deal on a load of his finest.

"You pick 'em out, and I'll haul 'em to the trailer," said my new Okie friend as we surveyed about five acres of melons. I really hated to admit to him that I didn't know beans about pickin' out watermelons, but he looked like an honest sort, so I told him that I didn't know a good one from a bad one until I cut it open, so I'd do the haulin', and he could do the pickin'.

"Just get me good ones." Dang it was hot, but we finally got the trailer loaded about four feet deep all the way to the back. We had on just under 5000 pounds. They cost me fifty cents apiece, and I headed 'er north with visions of bein' rich in a couple of days.

I was really surprised at the little woman's reaction. "You want me to do what? Not on your life cowboy! You bought 'em, you peddle 'em." It took some tall talkin' but I explained to her that we needed to use all the assets we had in the most efficient manner.

Somehow I managed to convince her that if she'd just sit by the highway in her white shorts and one of those little halter tops of her's that the customers would come flockin' to her door, and the watermelons would sell themselves. (She looks good in that kind of garb now, but you should have seen her thirty years ago.) All the compliments worked, and out to the highway she went.

The first day things went just about as I'd planned. She had sold about a third of the load, and other than being a little grouchy, like a true country girl, she had adjusted to the new challenge. It was all down hill from there. First, the bees and wasps found the treasure, and were getting really friendly with the smell of the melons. That didn't help her attitude any, but the last straw was the guy that squealed to a stop in a little red sports car.

He looks her up and down and says, "What'cha sellin' honey?" That was it. Over the edge she went.

"Watermelons you SOB!"

It is probably fortunate that I can't recall the exact exchange we had when she prematurely returned home. I just remember I lost, and wound up spendin' a couple of good hayin' days sittin' beside the highway pedalin' watermelons.

But then, all's well that ends well I guess, and we did manage to make about four hundred and fifty bucks on the deal. I still really don't understand.... if I looked like that in a halter top I'd be rich.

"That's it! I'm gettin' outa here!"

"Get back in the bunch, you two. It wasn't that bad!"

Chapter
Thirty-Two

Bunkhouse Ingenuity

Things are sure different than they used to be. When I was a kid there were lots of single men workin' on the farms and ranches, and living in the bunkhouse. These outfits used to be a lot more labor intensive than they are now, and I'm not so sure all this modern stuff is progress.

Most of those old boys must have died by now... at least they're certainly not as plentiful as they used to be. Back in the fifties most all of them were WW II vets, and for the most part good hard workers when they were workin', and durn hard drinkers the rest of the time. Some of them weren't good for over a couple of weeks, while others would last for several months before headin' into town to blow most (or all) of what they had comin'.

Our place wasn't any different than the rest, and Dad had his share of colorful characters. Ben Gooch didn't have a tooth in his head, and he was real ringer to say the least. Born in the hills of Tennessee, for some strange reason he found himself in jail in Hawaii the day Pearl Harbor was bombed.

Who knows what he did to get in that fix, but it must have been fairly serious, because when he was offered a full pardon to sign on with this new Ranger outfit that was being formed to go behind the Japanese lines in the South Pacific, he didn't even bat an eye. I guess he figured anything would be better than rottin' away in jail. The Good Lord must have been with him, because he was one of the few to make it back. I sure wish I could get a few of his stories now... they'd be worth a fortune.

Howard Larson was another guy that worked at our place for several years. He was a good hard worker, but like a lot of the others he drank up every dime he made. When he got too old to work and finally did retire, he came back to see us several times. He had been there so long that we were just like family to him. One of his favorite haunts on his time off was a little dive of a bar called Beanie's. That ol' place is history now too, but somehow Beanie managed to figure out a way to wind up with most of Howard's wages.

There was an unwritten law on every one of these outfits. "No booze in the bunkhouse." For the most part, it was fairly easy to spot any violators. They were fairly conspicuous consumers. It was pretty hard for most of them to drink in moderation.... in fact it was impossible.

A lot of the guys had nicknames that someone had hung on them. Pollock John was an old guy that worked on several of the outfits around here. He was tough as an ox, and his appetite for strong drink lacked many rivals, but his mental acuity left a little to be desired, so he was an obvious and enthusiastic candidate for "official experimental taster"... an office he held for several years.

He was working on a big ranch several miles from town, and with booze being outlawed in camp, he and some of the other boys were developin' a powerful thirst. Little Louie was the one with the idea.

"We should just get a little of that feed barely out of the bin and run us off some hooch."

There was another guy there they called Slick Tom. He was more than just a little skeptical, but like the others, hadn't had a drink for over two months, so was ready to be counted in. Louie assured the other two conspirators that he really did know how to make the stuff if they could just get their hands on a little yeast and a still. Discovery by the boss meant certain walkin' papers, but Tom volunteered to "borrow" the yeast out of the cookhouse, so they set out in earnest to scrounge up the materials they'd need for the still.

The yeast wasn't a problem. Slick Tom came through the very next day, and Little Louie got a batch of the barley and yeast brewin' in a five gallon bucket on the south side of the sheep shed in the sun. The still proved a little harder to come by. The best they could come up with for something to boil the mash in was an old galvanized chicken waterer.

"Dat von't verk!" says Pollock John, "Dat galfanisin' on dat ting vill kill you!"

"Naw, it won't," retorted Tom, "I seen guys do that lots of times."

Rumor has it that copper is the preferred metal for that sort of thing, but availability was a real problem. They couldn't even seem to find a chunk of copper tubing that was near long enough to make the coil. The best they could do was an old chunk of gas line, but it was way too short. They looked high and low for days, but kept coming up empty handed.

The boys were getting thirstier by the minute, and Little Louie said the mash was ready, so they were forced to improvise.

"Let's just cut a chunk off that hose we water the horses with," suggested Tom.

"Ya, dat vill verk," answered Pollock John, lickin' his lips. He headed right down to the barn to cut six or eight feet off the rubber hose by the horse trough.

They found a place in the willows behind the barn that was out of sight of the big house to build a fire, and punched a hole in the top of the chicken waterer for the hose. Tom found a little tar to seal up the hole real tight, and Louie filled the contraption with the precious mash, and they set it on the fire, waiting impatiently for the miraculous result. Pollock John made a big coil out of the rubber hose, and hung it up on the willows just like they told him and nervously held a Mason jar under the end, constantly lickin' his lips.

They didn't have to wait too long. Soon, between the smoke from the fire and the steam from the leaks in the chicken waterer, they caught their first glimpse of the precious liquid. One little drip at a time...

"Here she comes!" yelled Tom.

"Sshhtt! Pipe down Slick, they'll hear you hollarin'!" cautioned Little Louie, looking over his shoulder.

Just then a big black blowfly landed on the Mason jar, being obviously attracted by the overpowering aroma. There was now nearly a half an inch of the new hooch in the jar bottom, and the fly started a nice leisurely stroll around the rim. He only got about half way around when he fell over dead on his back on the ground. He never kicked a foot.

"I tol you dat galfanisin' stuff vould kill you! Yust look at dat!" said Pollock John emphatically.

"Naw, it won't, John," answered Tom, "he was prob'ly sick anyway. It looks OK to me. Give 'er a try, see how she tastes."

Pollock John barely hesitated. He shut his eyes and licked his lips one last time, and slapped back a

140

big swig, his huge shoulders shuddering as he swallowed.

"Acht! It tastes yust like gum boots!" said the big man gasping for air, "....but I tink she's OK." Then he turned her bottoms up for another pull.

I'm not certain if they drank the rest of that concoction or not. It really could have been poison, I don't know..... but, now come to think of it, I haven't seen any of those ol' boys for a while.

S-B Headquarters in the '70s
The prairie fire of '91 burned it to the ground.

Note: October 16, 1991 is a day that will forever be seared upon the hearts and minds of all who happened to be anywhere near Blaine County in northern Montana. A lightning caused fire, driven by gale force winds raced across nearly 150 thousand acres, leaving behind only the charred remains of farms and ranches and their attendant dreams. Over three hundred head of livestock were lost, and in excess of 150 ranch buildings, including many homes were completely destroyed. Only the hand of the Good Lord himself kept the death toll from being even higher. The S-B was one of the many unfortunate places that laid directly in the path the day "all hell broke loose".

The "Great Fire of '91" was itself the subject of an entire book. Fire In The Wind was published in 1994 by the Milk River Genealogical Society.

Chapter Thirty-Three

The Sheepherdin' Cow Boss

I rode for the S-B Ranch the spring of '72. It was calvin' time, and Fritz agreed to put me on. Fritz Helmle had been the foreman there for many years, and I suppose he was in his 60s someplace. Whenever I think of Fritz, the first thing that comes to mind is his great big smile, and his thick German accent.

He was a workin' fool, always on the go, and had a way of gettin' more out of a man than anyone I ever knew. I think he was 19 or 20 when he came over from Germany to work for the Kuhr Ranch. He was always quick to tell me he was "bossin'" for Kuhrs. I guess that was to clear up any confusion . . . . so I'd know he wasn't just a regular hand.

I can't say that I've ever had a better boss. He was always encouragin' the crew and urging them on, but workin' for Fritz was also a real challenge for a

143

cowboy. You see, he was a sheep man. He'd been with the big outfits when they ran mostly sheep, and when they made the transition to cattle....well, Fritz came along, but I really think his heart was still in the sheep business.

Sheep and cattle are similar in a lot of ways, but there are a few pretty significant differences. Therein enters the frustration. Let me tell you about a time that will help show you how he could be frustratin' and encouraging at the same time.

It was the last part of April sometime, and it was time to get some cows paired up and ready to go to the range north of the river. Warner Ramberg was the regular cowboy there, and a good hand he was, too. They had a couple of other guys doin' the feeding, and one calvin' the heifers, so that left Warner and I to do the ridin'.

He was a good pard to ride with. If he wasn't in the right place at the right time, it dang shore wasn't his fault. Warner was up on the ridge gettin' in a cow that needed some attention, and Fritz had this "little job" for me. Superman couldn't have done that "little job".

He had this brainy idea for me to go out into a pasture, and cut out a couple of loads of pairs, (about 80 head) and trail em' through another field of cows and calves, then put them into the pasture where they'd be ready to ship up north. I was tryin' to think of a real diplomatic way to break the news to him that it'd be totally impossible for one man to do that by him- self, when before I could begin my protest, he started braggin' on my mount, and tellin' me what a heck of a hand I was, and about how he wished he looked as good on a horse as I did.

My hat started gettin' tight as my head began to swell, and the whole time I was thinkin', "You're right Fritz. I am one heck of a hand. No normal man could do that, but I ain't normal." He had me convinced I could do anything.

As his pickup rattled over the hill, and my head shrank back to it's regular size, the realization hit me that my pride was at stake now. Fritz thinks I can do the impossible, and I don't dare let him down.

Well, I tied into that unattainable goal, and in the process, durn near ran my horse plumb to death. I'd just get a few pairs separated, and they'd try to get back in the main bunch again. It was an impossible assignment, but then I wasn't just any old cowboy. I was way better than most, in

Warner Ramberg, A Dang Good Cowboy

fact, I just might be the best hand that ever lived....Fritz had just told me so, and like a fool I'd believed him.

I was just beginnin' to feel like General Custer, when over the hill loped my fathful ol' Pard. I was never so glad to see help comin' in my life. It's just plain amazin' what the two best hands on earth can do when they're teamed up. We knew for sure we were, 'cause Fritz told us that almost everyday.

In no time we had the two loads of pairs cut out and headed down the fence. We were takin' our time to make sure the Mamas didn't loose track of their babies, and visey-versey. We managed to evade the bunch of cows in the field we had to pass through, and were closin' in on the gate to our destination pasture, when over the hill charges Fritz to the rescue.

I know he thought he was doin' us a big favor by opening the gate, but we'd both been prayin' he wouldn't show up. Herein lies the main difference between movin' cows and sheep. With cows and calves, the secret is keepin' 'em paired up. With sheep, it isn't that big a deal, as they tend to stay in a bunch anyway, and they'll find their babies sooner or later. But sheep need a leader, and by George, Fritz was gonna make sure they had one.

He opens the gate, and jumps in the back of his pickup and yells at the cows to follow him. After all, he'd been feedin' 'em cake all winter, and they just loved that thick German "come boooooss". And "come boooooss" they did. He was beatin' his scoop shovel on the pickup box and callin' and throwin' out a little cake now and then. For just a fraction of a second we had a half a stampede goin'.

The cow half of our herd stampeded straight toward their favorite German, and the calf half just stopped dead in their tracks, tryin' to figure out what was goin' on. They all seemed to figure it out at the same time. To a calf they were completely convinced in their pointed little bovine heads that their Mamas must be back where they sucked last....about two miles ago.

That's when the second half of the stampede started. Only problem was, it was in the wrong direction. If you've ever tried to chase a bunch of calves one way when they are completely convinced their mothers are in the other direction, then you have an idea of what we were up against. It's sorta like tryin' to chase a flock of chickens when you're horseback. It was a real wreck. Somehow we managed to get the job done.... but then what else could you expect from the two best cowboys that ever lived.

Fritz is gone now, and I sure miss him. Ever'body needs a little encouragement now and then, and he was the best.

Chapter Thirty-Four

Cow Checkin' Fer Dummies

Ahh, spring... when a young man's fancy turns to love. The bulls get pretty durn hard to keep in, too. An ol' boy told me once that he thought that those two deals were related somehow.... I'll be doggoned.

All the calvin' takes place around here in the spring, and it sure can get to be an interesting time of the year. Although most everyone looks forward to it, it does get to wearin' on the old body some.

Now, there is a secret to checkin' cows in the middle of the night. I don't share my secrets too often, but this one is a pivotal part of spring survival on a cow outfit, so I feel sort of compelled to let ever'one else in on it. Probably 95% of the time, you get up for nothin'. Either there isn't anything goin' on, or you wait up for some heifer, and she calves by herself anyway.

So through the years, I've almost perfected the

art of "sleep walkin' cow checkin'". After a nice little midnight walk out to the shed, there ain't nothin' worse than climbin' back in bed and starin' two eyed at the ceiling at 2AM (or one eyed, in my case) and not bein' able to go back to sleep.

This little plan of mine works most of the time, but on one particular occasion a few years back, me and my blushin' bride were fresh married, and things didn't turn out too good. It was the middle of March, and I got up to check the cows. Even at that tender young age she was a little ouchy about gettin' woke up in the middle of the night, so it's in my own best interest to try to just doze through the check, and just maybe I could go back to sleep, too. I got up and pulled on my jeans and a coat, grabbed the flashlight, and headed out the door. I'd gotten in the habit of not even buttoning my jeans. I'd just hold them up with one hand. It's a lot faster.

We had quite a bit of snow that spring, so we had all the cows in the corrals with a big old straw pile mounded up in the middle of it. It had chinook'd, and the snow was all gone, but the only dry place for the old girls to calve was on that straw pile. The rest of the pen was a soupy mixture of melted snow and the remains of digested hay. Pee soup. The soup was about six inches deep, with a nice layer of ice underneath it, which made things slicker than the dickens, and the walkin' a little tricky. Ever' once in a while a cow would crawl off in a corner to be by herself, and would drop a calf in the soup, so they had to be checked pretty regular.

I'm doin' my usual sleep walkin' routine. Shufflin' though the slop to the straw pile. One eye is plumb shut, and the other one is only half open, and I'm holdin' up my jeans with my left had and shinin' the light around with my right one. Everything seems to be normal; no calves in the slop, so I headed up on the straw mound to see if there was anything new up there.

The old milk cow had calved the day before, and we'd been too busy to look him over very well. She was layin' beside him right on the edge of the straw, so just to make sure he'd had a suck and was ok, I gave him a kick as I went by just to see how lively he was.

I sure wish I hadn't done that. He let out a beller, as they sometimes do, and jumped to his feet. He's fine, I thought to myself. Nope, his mama wasn't any problem. She was gentle as a kitten, but there was another old bag there that was just fixin' to calve that was claimin' him. That led to a real problem. They'll do that sometimes, you know. Nobody on earth really understands them female hormone deals for sure, but sometimes the motherin' hormone kicks in before calf havin' hormone is plumb done, and the old girls will "granny". They'll claim a calf that's already born, swearin' to goodness it's their own.

That is precisely what happened on that fateful night, and the cow doin' the "grannyin'" was the worst old ring tail on the place. She let out a bawl and hit me right in the middle of the chest with her head. I did a nearly perfect reverse swan dive off the edge of the straw, landin' flat on my back in six inches of thirty degree pee soup, and takin' about fifteen feet to skid to a stop. I was purty well awake by now, and must not have my divin' technique completely perfected because somehow I lost the hold I had on my jeans, and they wound up around my knees someplace with 20 pounds of the awfulest smellin' stuff you ever saw in the seat of 'em. Pull 'em up or take 'em off? I had my overshoes on so up they came....fillin' my boots.

Surprisin' as it may seem, I still recommend the "walkin' in yer sleep" method of cow checkin'. That ol' bed shore felt good after shovelin' out my jeans, and dumpin' out my boots, and the shower drain only plugged up a couple of times.

Dang it, but I can't remember if the cook got woke up or not.

Chapter Thirty-Five

Fast Thinkin' Rodney

I just got to thinkin' today about some of the excuses that I've heard. Kids have a way of comin' up with some dillys. I can remember gettin' pretty creative a time or two when I was in a jam, but one of the best ones I ever did hear turned out to be the truth.....but then they say truth is stranger than fiction.

If there was ever a kid that was in trouble over at the Willow Creek School, it was Slow Johnson. His real name was Rodney, but he did everything about half speed, so got tagged with the name Slow. He walked slow, he talked slow, in fact, he did everything slow....except think. He could talk his way out of just about anything. Maybe it was because he got so much practice. He was one of the younger Johnson kids, and in that outfit a kid had to be a thinker just to survive. He was a red headed, freckle faced little nubbin of a kid, sort of small for his age, and usually wore patched

151

up old overalls that had been handed down about three times before they got down to him. It seemed like his shirt tail was always out, and trouble just seemed to follow him around. He was continually in some kind of a jam.

The Johnsons lived on a gumbo flat that wouldn't grow much but greasewood and kids. The folks were good hard workers, but they didn't have much of a chance. They were poor as snakes. There were a lot of kids to feed and times were hard back then. One October morning it was almost time for the morning recess when Slow finally came mopin' into the school house. Miss Blackstone lit into him pretty hard.

"Rodney, do you know what time it is? You are two hours late for school. This behavior is unacceptable."

In his usual slow manner, Rodney began to explain, "'Taint my fault Miss Blackstone."

Accustomed to his wild imagination, the teacher was prepared for the worst. "Well then exactly who is

The Old Collins School on the Teton River
(Slow Johnson never went here.)

152

responsible?"

"'Taint sure Ma'am, but its either my Pa's or Ol' Sounder's. You see Pa don't put on no pajamas when he goes to bed, an' Ol' Sounder is gettin' real hard of hearin'. Sounder is our dog, you know. Or maybe its the coon's fault for gettin' in the chicken coop, but it shore ain't my fault."

Miss Blackstone was torn between immediate punishment for poor ol' Slow, and a deferred sentence, but her curiosity necessitated hearing the remainder of his tale. "Ain't isn't a word, Rodney. Perhaps you had better tell me the whole story. Quickly, please."

"Yes, Ma'am," Slow began...slower than ever. "Well, there's been this coon gettin in the chicken coop, and Pa heard this awful squawkin' in the middle of the night, so he got the shotgun and headed outside. He was in a real hurry, so he didn't even stop to pull his britches on or nuthin'. He was crawlin' on his hands and knees up to the coop as quiet as a mouse, and just about had the coon in his sights, when the commotion finally got loud enough that it woke up Ol' Sounder."

"He could tell right away that there was a critter in the chicken coop, and in the dark I guess he musta thought that Pa was the critter. Pa was just fixin' to cut down on the coon when Ol' Sounder tied into the back end of what he thought was the critter. You see, Miss Blackstone, 'taint my fault," Slow concluded as he dramatically wiped some sleep from his eyes, "'cause we been up cleanin' chickens since three o'clock this mornin'."

Now that's an excuse.

"Personally, I don't believe a word this guy says."

Chapter

Thirty-Six

Better Check Yer Shoes

Chuck and Mary Ellen are just your normal kind of northern plains country folks. They've run a farm and ranch combination outfit all of their lives, and just this last year turned it over to one of the boys to see just how long it would take him to starve his kids to death on it. Mary Ellen was all into travelin'. After all, they'd put in their time, and they needed to give the kids a little room.

"Let's get us a fifth wheel trailer and go down south for the winter," Mary Ellen suggested with palm trees dancing in her eyes.

"Nuthin' doin!" was Chuck's compassionate reply. "Those durn things cost a fortune. Besides, I ain't about to hang around on one of those cock-eyed southern sand piles covered up with tin shacks full of old people as far as you can see in ever' direction. What a waste of time."

In about a month they were headed south. I guess it's fairly easy to see who won that argument. Chuck was determined he wasn't going to have a good time, and grumbled all the way to Arizona. He sat in the trailer and pouted for two or three weeks while Mary Ellen had the time of her life. She had taken up crocheting a couple of years before, and after meeting several ol' girls with the same interest, had a pile of friends in nothin' flat. Chuck was still poutin', but finally came to the conclusion that she wasn't going to let him go home anyway, so he'd just as well make the best of it.

The guy in the trailer next to theirs asked him to go along to one of the little Mexican border towns, and he reluctantly accepted the invitation. To his surprise, he actually had a pretty good time. There were little street shops everywhere, and bargains galore. He and Mary Ellen decided to take different streets to check out the shops, and agreed to meet at a bench in the town square in an hour.

Chuck got back to the meeting place a little early, and waited.....and waited.....and waited. Finally after two hours he was nearly worried out of his head. The very worst scenarios were playing out in his mind, as he made his way through the crowded streets to the police station to report his missing wife.

"Can you geeve me a deescription pleeze?" the helpful policeman asked. Of course Chuck gave him all the vital information, including what she was wearing.

"Sir, I am afraid we have theese lady in custodeee," the policeman said as he took on a sudden air of importance.

"Custody?" yelled Chuck. Then seeing the policeman bristle, quickly lowered his voice. "What in the world for?"

"I'm afraid she was soleeciting weeth out a license."

"Ain't this just my luck," thought Chuck to himself, "eighteen hundred miles from home, and here my ol' lady gets busted for tryin' to peddle crocheted doilies in Mexico. You can get the durn things down here cheaper than you can buy the yarn. What in the dickens is the matter with that woman anyway?"

His train of thought took a sudden left turn as the policeman continued, "Een our country we take prostitution veery seeriously, and soleeciting weethout a license ees never permitted."

"Prostitution? Mary Ellen? There must be some mistake officer. She might try hockin' a doily now and then, but this is ridiculous."

"Oh no Sir, eet ees no meestake. See for yourself. She hass on red shoess. Een thees country only prostitutes wear red shoess," the policeman said sternly.

"If yer gonna be solicitin', then you gotta have a license. Makes sense to me."

Arguin' didn't get poor old Chuck anywhere. There was Mary Ellen in a foreign country charged with a crime, and still wearing two feet full of evidence.

"I knew we should o' stayed back up home," Chuck muttered under his breath. "What must I do to clear this up officer?" he then continued aloud as politely as he could.

"Soleeciting weeth out a license ees a fine of seventy five U.S. doolars," came the answer as the policeman rubbed his hands together, "of course eef you care to abide by thee law and buy her a license, we can forgeet thees ever happened." Seeing the question marks where Chuck's eyes used to be, he continued, "We can geeve her a license for one yeeer for forty U.S. doolars."

157

"We'll take the license," was the immediate reply, "Wait 'til the folks back in Williston hear about this one."

Mary Ellen was a little miffed. For some strange reason she felt her honor had been violated, but was certainly very careful about the shoes she wore to Mexico after that. As a matter of fact, I think she burned the old ones that got her in the jam.

Chuck? He's having a great time down there now, and proudly displays Mary Ellen's license on the trailer wall. "You just need a sense of humor, Mama. Besides, I saved us thirty five bucks . . . . and," he continued laughin' under his breath, "I've got the only licensed prostitute in the whole campground."

Uh-Oh!

Chapter Thirty-Seven

Cookie Stealin' Crowe

*D*id you ever take time to think about the nicknames that folks get tagged with? Maybe some sections of the country are a little worse for hangin' a new name on a feller than others. I think ever' Indian friend I have has one. We've got some kinfolk in the Ozarks, and they've all got 'em, too. Dump, Dabber, Gabby, and Stub are just a few that come driftin' across my mind.

One time one of my little brothers wrote a letter to an uncle just addressed; "Uncle Muck, Mountain View, Missouri". Yea, it got there. He'd been called Muck so long that nobody knew what his real name was.

A neighbor of ours got a new handle at our place a few years ago. Bob Crowe had bought a place that bordered ours, and came into the yard one day to see about borrowin' a piece of machinery. He hadn't been in the neighborhood too long, and we just barely knew each other. He was a big raw boned long armed feller, and as his wife worked in town, he didn't get a whole lot to eat that he didn't scrounge up himself.

My little woman is from the old school, and it's a cinch nobody leaves the place hungry. She always cooks about twice as much as she needs to just in case somebody like ol' Bob happens in the yard about meal time.

She came out and hollers, "Get washed up. It's almost ready."

Gettin' him to stay for dinner didn't take much arm twistin', 'cause I'm purty sure he hadn't had a square meal for a week or so. I don't think he'd ever been inside our house before, and in her usual style, the cook sets the table like she was expectin' a thrashin' crew. She had a big roast beef and mashed potatoes and all the trimmin's.

Now I'm tellin' ya that boy could eat. He kinda reminded me of a half starved coyote that happens on to a dead cow and trys to finish her off in one meal. 'Course the cook was in her height 'n glory, and ever' time ol' Bob's plate would start 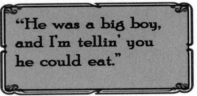 gettin' a little low she'd start the stuff around again. He'd just pile the grub on, and tell her how great it was, and she'd wiggle like a little puppy and pass him somethin' else. I didn't think he was ever gonna get filled up.

The last time the meat and taters went around, with a little extra encouragement from the cook, he almost took more than he could eat. As Granny used to say, "His eyes durn near got too big for his belly." He'd had a good fetchin' up, and was as long on manners as he was on appetite, so he wasn't about to leave anything on his plate. He had quite a struggle, and it took him a while, but he finally got around the last of it. I'm sure he musta felt just like that ol' coyote when the cow was all gone. He was just plain miserable.

We'd had quite a visit during dinner, and hadn't even noticed that the little woman had whipped up a batch of chocolate chip cookies while we were eatin'. She's always bustlin' around in the kitchen doin' something. She opens the oven, and flips four or five nice fresh hot ones on Bob's plate. The sight of food just didn't seem to have the same appeal to him it had a half an hour earlier. He was too polite to tell her he was about to bust and couldn't hold another bite, even though she didn't even give him a chance to pass.

He got this plan. If he could just take a couple of little nibbles, and then slip the cookies into his pocket when no one was lookin', then the cook wouldn't get offended, and there would be a little somethin' left for later on. It was a purty good idea, and it would have worked if it hadn't been for one of the kids. One of our little rug rats was just walkin' and talkin' good. He comes around a corner, stops right in the middle of the kitchen, points at our guest, and says in a shrill two year old voice, "Hey, look! Bob Crowe is puttin' cookies in his pocket!"

Needless to say he was nearly embarrassed to tears, and carried the handle "Cookie Stealin' Crowe" 'til the day he died.

"Now this next deal is plumb the truth. I was lookin' over the fence, an' I saw the whole thing."

Chapter Thirty-Eight

Hot Dang

*T*he guys that write all those cartoon books and draw all the pictures on the calendars of those goofy lookin' cowboys in the old rattle trap outfits owe me a fortune in royalties. I think they've been followin' me around and makin' big bucks by just drawin' pictures of what they've seen happen to me.

It's just plain unfair that they should be spendin' the winter on some South Sea island and living in leisure while I'm haulin' hay and chopin' water holes in the Milk River with the cold east wind blowin' up my shirt tail. I know nobody said life was fair, but it still ain't right.

It sure isn't on purpose that my life turns out like a page out of a joke book....but by George it seems to. Now, just take last fall for instance. We were tearin' down some old corrals out behind the barn. I think some of 'em had been there before the homestead days, and because it was back where you don't drive by it ever' day, it was a real mess. There was at least a hundred years worth of old poles and posts and wire layin' around back there. One nice Indian summer afternoon, there was quite a crew around here just doin' nothin', and someone got the bright idea to clean some of that mess up. I was all for it.

We found an old ditch that would be a good safe place to start a fire, and started throwin' that old junk in. Boy, were we spiffin' the place up. It got to be too far to drag everything, so somebody started up the old truck, and when the box got full, they'd putt down by the fire and hoist it off, and somebody else would push the mess in with the loader. We kept that fire goin' for a couple of days, and things started lookin' a whole lot better.

As is usually the case with projects like that, the new wore off before the job was done, and ever'body got busy doing somethin' else. It was a nice calm evenin' just before supper, and I got the brainy idea to crank that old fire up again. I drug a few old chunks of stuff over and throwed 'em on the coals, and before long, the flames were ten feet high again.

Ever'thing was goin' according to the plan until I went over to get the load that was left on the truck. I hadn't been runnin' the truck before, bein' the boss and all, but now there wasn't anyone else around. The battery ain't the best in the old girl, but she started right up, and we headed for the fire. Now, ever'body else had dumped the truck beside the ditch, and pushed the old boards in with the tractor, but bein' a thinker like I am, it looked way more efficient to just back 'er down and dump 'er right in the fire.

There's a nice little slope down to the ditch, and I'm backin' this old truck down to the fiery inferno. The mirror's busted, so I had to look between all the little cracks with my one eyeball to see where I was goin'. (Ever'body thinks a cowboy's life is easy.) Oh, I could see where I was goin' OK, cracks and all, but needin' to save a little time, and not wantin' to have to start the tractor, I figgered if I'd back right up to the ditch bank with the back wheels, then I could hoist the load of junk right into the flames.

This even sounds like a good plan now. It would o' worked too, if I'd had any brakes. Nope, no brakes. The pedal went right to the floor. (That musta been the reason they didn't back down the hill.) Oh, I got 'er stopped all right, after a half a dozen good pumps, but the back wheels were over the ditch bank. I jammed the gear shift into compound low and popped the clutch.... and killed 'er. That ol' battery is only good for one start, so there I was. The load's on fire. (Can you see the cartoon yet?)

I'm a good thinker under pressure. I think maybe it's because my entire life has been pressurized. I must be gettin' used to it. The tractor was close, and there was a chain on the back, so I made a run for it. The fire is gainin' on me now, and half the load's in flames. I hooked 'er up, and jerked her up the hill a ways. Now we have two fires... one where its 'sposed to be, and one in the back of the truck.

This is where my new guardian angel took over, probably out of pity. I say new angel because I'm sure they have to be rotated on a regular basis. An Overcast guardian angel has his work cut out for him, and because of the stress, the burn out rate is fairly high. That is the only explanation, because when I jumped back in the ol' truck, she started right up. That durn battery will never start it more than once.

Boy, things are goin' my way now. I dumped the load, jammed the old girl in gear, and headed for the water hydrant. The mud flaps and the back of the box were in flames, but it was only about a hundred yards or so to the hose. The motor was wrapped up pretty tight, and I was just gettin' ready to ketch another gear, when... **Kerpow!** The side of my head durn near

165

busted out the side window, and we came to a sudden stop. I musta ran over something. I couldn't remember anything being in front of me, but maybe I didn't look too good, bein' in sort of a hurry and all.

Well, it didn't take a brain surgeon to see the problem. I was still hooked up to the tractor. I had no idea that old truck could get up to 25 miles an hour in the length of the 20 foot log chain. It's a dang wonder I didn't jerk the front axle plumb off it.

I hosed the fire out, and other than some crispy mud flaps, and the burnt off wires to the tail lights that didn't work anyway, the only real damage was a scorched ten year old license plate, and a big knot above my left ear.

I'm tellin' ya, those guys owe me a fortune.

Chapter
Thirty-Nine

PU in the Pew

*W*e're out of grass, out of water, out of money, out of hay, out of credit, out of energy, and there isn't an outfit on the place that will run. Other than that, things seem to be going pretty good around here.

There isn't anything wrong on this outfit that a foot of rain and a couple of million bucks wouldn't fix. I can't ever remember workin' so hard and gettin' less done. Oh well, it comes with the territory I guess. It isn't much consolation, but we definitely aren't alone. The cows are rollin' out of this neck of the woods so fast it's hard to count the trucks. Everyone knows this is officially a semi-arid country, but this is ridiculous.

It seems like this dry stuff just gets passed around from one area to the other. They had a big drought down in the Sand Hills country a few years ago, and things got a little rough on the Williams' outfit that year, too. Charlie and Bertha had been in business for quite a few years, and it was back before they switched to runnin' yearlings.

They had a whole mess of cows and calves, and it was just about this time of year. They were busy hauling water and hay, and chasin' starvin' cows, and were just about to the end of their rope. I guess the shear exhaustion is what started it all, but overwork and a lack of sleep can do strange things to the old body. Charlie would fall asleep at the drop of a hat, and it got to be a real habit. It was sort of like takin' a nap after dinner, once you get a deal like that started, it's an easy rut to get into, but she's pretty tough to get back out.

For the most part it was harmless. He stayed awake most of the time when he was drivin', but the real rub came when they went to church. Those old hard oak church pews didn't bother ol' Charlie a bit. He was out like a light long before the preachin' started.

It wouldn't have been so bad if he hadn't snored. Bertha was embarrassed to tears, and was at her wit's end, so she secretly sought the preacher's council. Now the pastor was a wizened old gent that had been to college and everything. He understood perfectly that Charlie was near total exhaustion, and assured Bertha that Charlie's behavior wouldn't at all affect his status with his Maker.

"But it's so embarrassing," pled Bertha, "isn't there something that can be done? Please help me!"

"I have only seen one cure for this sort of thing," replied the wise old cleric. "There has to be a jolt to the inner most sections of Charlie's brain. We must somehow convince his subconscious to relate a very unpleasant experience with his church sleeping habits. Positive results will only be achieved by an extreme and very traumatic shock to his subconscious."

His advice was to hide a well-wrapped piece of Limburger cheese deep within Bertha's purse, and to thrust it under Charlie's nose when he nodded off next Sunday.

"His subconscious will then relate the terrible smell with falling asleep in church, and it will prevent this type of thing from ever happening again. I've seen it work many times before."

Bertha was willing to try anything, so the very next Sunday, she wrapped a large piece of very ripe Limburger cheese in tin foil and concealed it in her purse. One thing was for sure, ol' Charlie was predictable. Right after the first song, he was out like a light again, snores and all. His life long helpmate, eager to end her embarrassment, quietly removed the odoriferous sleep dissuader from its hiding place, quickly removed the wrapping, and thrust it directly under her hubby's sunburned nose.

Things unfortunately went from bad to worse. Charlie stood straight up in the old oak church pew and growled loudly, "For cryin' out loud, Bertha…. get your feet off my pillow!"

"I know, I know.... but keep readin'. The boss needs the work."

Chapter Forty

Petrified Profit

*D*ick and Billy are back in the chips again....
... in more ways than one. They've kinda put their
Tomcat neuterin' business on hold for the time being.
Besides, the marketing got to be a real hassle after
Mrs. Sullivan spread the word around that she was
absolutely certain they didn't know what they were
doing.

Their botched job had really gotten her Irish up
when her poor little Tommy came bounding back home
across the CRP with that terrified look in his eye. She
had to put her little baby in counseling for weeks, and
then blabbed her big mouth all over the county. As a
result the business just sort of dried up. Now, those
boys aren't the type to give up easy.... but then it really
doesn't matter anymore. They've got a way better deal
goin' now. It all started when Billy was gathering the
bulls up by Adobe Butte and came back with this funny

lookin' rock that he used to prop the bunkhouse door open.

"Where'd you get that dumb rock, anyway?" asked Dick as he scanned over the newspaper.

"Up there on the side of 'dobe Butte," was Billy's reply, "There's a whole bunch of 'em up there. Weird lookin' ain't it?" Right then Dick... the thinker, gave an excited yell.

"Whoopee! Look-ee here pardner!" He exclaimed pointin' one crooked finger at the newspaper. "I'll betcha a nickel this is what that durn rock is!"

The article in the paper was about some enterprising folks that were marketing petrified dinosaur do-do. The stuff's got an official name, but I'll be durned if I can remember what it is.

"We can make a killin' sellin' those things," Dick yelled excitedly. "We can get one of those big blow-up dinosaurs, and tear a few windbreak boards off the corral behind the barn to make us a roadside stand, and...."

"Dad-blame it Dick!" Interrupted Billy as he opened one of Milwaukee's finest for breakfast, "That's the most hair-brained idea you've ever come up with. What sort of a crazy fool would buy somthin' like that?"

"The same kind of a fool that tries to run us over ever' time we get out on the highway with a piece of machinery.... the durn tourists, Dummy. Anybody that ain't bright enough to tell that the swather on the road ahead of 'em isn't goin' eighty miles an hour ought to be an easy target for a sale...don'tcha think? Nope, I'm not kiddin'. It says right here in the paper that people actually buy that stuff. Besides, we haven't got any hay to cut anyway. We don't have a thing to lose but a little time."

"Ain't you got any pride at all? I've got my principles, you know," hiccupped Billy. "No self respectin' cowboy would be caught dead out on the highway in a roadside stand peddlin' dinosaur droppin's. Besides, we ain't even sure that's what that stuff is."

"Dang it, Billy. It don't matter if that ain't what it is. As long as the dumb tourists **THINK** that's what it is, that's all that counts."

"Now that's not exactly honest Dick, and you know it. What would yer Mama.... rest her soul... think of you sellin' funny lookin' rocks as some kind of petrified artifact?" Dick wasn't ever accused of being the most honest guy west of the Mississippi. Although he never did lie, he was known to get a little reckless with the truth on occasion.

"That **MIGHT** be what those rocks are. Besides, **NOBODY** but the dinosaur is gonna know for sure anyway. You finish that barley sandwich and go back up on the Butte and get a couple of five gallon buckets of that stuff, and I'll rip off some wind break boards and we'll give 'er a try."

The very next morning they had their stand set up out on the blacktop road at the edge of town. They had even gotten themselves a big rubber dinosaur filled with helium, and had it tied to the pickup bumper with a lariat rope. Now, that took a little experimentation. The first time they just put the rope around his neck, (cowboy logic) but the durn thing was floatin' butt up.... that would never do. Tying it around one hind foot seemed to work a whole lot better.

Dick was in charge of marketing, while Billy was in the procurement department. (He was up on the Butte pickin' rock.) This new plan worked like a charm. The only problem was that business was so good that the demand was startin' to outstrip the supply. That was until Dick (he's the thinker) fixed the problem. He went into town and invested in two German Shepherds and a microwave oven. I wish I'da thought of that.

Montana Cowboys... they work hard & eat good.
circa 1890's

Chapter Forty-One

Murder at the Bear Paw Wagon

*T*here's an old tombstone in the cemetery up on the hill north of town that has interested me for years. It's a big one for as old as it is. Here's what it reads:

Frank M. Mitchell
Cowboy
Wantonly shot by a companion in roundup
camp near Snake Butte.
October 17, 1898
Honest, earnest, generous, and kind.
He merited life and joy.

I've been walkin' past that old stone since I was a kid, and always wondered about it. I'm a real sucker for old cowboy stories, and true ones are even better. "Someday I'm goin' to check into that," I told myself....but of course I never did. Life sure seems to stay hectic, doesn't it?

Well, last winter I finally took the time and looked into it a little bit. I went to the library here in town and they helped me dig up some old copies of the Chinook Opinion, one of the newspapers of the day, and I even stopped in at the Court House in Fort Benton, and looked into some of the old court records. There were a lot fewer counties around then, and this area was part of Choteau county with the seat bein' about 100 miles away. Now that was a fer piece when horseback was the main mode of transportation.

It seems Frank was the cook on one of the chuck wagons of the Bear Paw Pool. The Bear Paw Pool was an association of stockmen from this part of the state, with a range extending from the Missouri River on the south to the Canadian border on the north and spanning 150 miles or so in width. The country was all open range. It must have been a sight to see. The wagon was camped on Snake Creek in an area described as "the cottonwoods" about six or eight miles northwest of Snake Butte, and approximately ten miles downstream from the Nez Perce battlefield where "the last great Indian battle" had been fought some twenty years previous.

Besides Frank, the cook, there were three other men in camp on that fateful Monday morning. Captain Frank Plunkett was in charge of the roundup crew which was out on the morning circle. An altercation ensued between the well liked cook and a drifter from Wyoming named J.C Baldwin.

The details of the argument are a little sketchy, but it apparently concluded when Frank slapped Baldwin who went into the cook tent and sat down to pout for a few minutes. When he returned a short time later, he was carrying a pistol belonging to Jack Emerson, who was out ridin' the circle.

Poor old Frank was peelin' potatoes for the noon meal. Baldwin cussed him and fired the pistol three times at point blank range. Only one of the shots hit its mark with the others goin' wild. One bullet hit the cook just below the right eye and lodged in the back of his neck. Baldwin then ran to the horse corral and takin' one of the Pool horses headed for parts unknown, ridin' like his life depended on it.....and I'm sure it did.

John Matheson was one of the two men who witnessed the whole affair. He rode to the Fort Belknap Indian Agency, about five or six miles to the north east, and brought back a doctor who bandaged the wounds.

John was a respected witness, and had a place in the Milk River Valley near the North Fork siding of the Great Northern Railroad.

When Captain Plunkett and the cowboys returned from the roundup later in the day, Mitchell was loaded in a wagon and transported to Chinook, a distance of seventeen some odd miles. I'll bet that wagon trip didn't feel too good on that fresh headache. Frank Mitchell lived a little over a week, then died of a severe hemorrhage after a coughing spell. He was laid to rest, and the Bear Paw Pool boys raised the money for his stone.

There are a couple of things that really intrigued me about this old story. First, by coincidence, the roundup camp was most likely located on what is now our summer range. My Granddad and one of his brothers bought a chunk of ground on Snake Creek in the 1940's, and it's location sure matches where the killin' took place. And second, according to the court records I uncovered in Fort Benton, the case is still open.

There was a warrant issued for Baldwin's arrest, but he was never brought to justice. The case was finally dropped from the court docket several years later with instructions that it would be opened again in the event of an arrest. It never was. J.C. Baldwin was never brought to trial, leaving his fate to our imagination.

We do know that J.C. rode to Clear Creek and got his own horse, a bay branded 9-6 on the left thigh, and pulled out taking the pistol belonging to Jack Emerson. The whole country was in an uproar, as Mitchell was not only a good cook, but a good guy, and the roundup boys had blood in their eye.

Did he make it across the Missouri and head for points south never to return? In the days before social security numbers and computers it sure was a whole lot easier to just change your name and start over. It's entirely possible that he lived out his life under another identity. 'Course there's probably nobody alive now that would know for sure, but I have my own theory.

The Cottonwoods & Snake Butte

I think he got his just reward from some of Frank Mitchell's cowboy friends. He more than likely got his neck stretched with his own rope, or ran into the business end of one or more Winchesters. Justice came swiftly in those days. It ain't no wonder the law couldn't find him.

If there are some Baldwins in your family tree, it might be wise not to check into all this too close.

Chapter Forty-Two

Precipitable Encouragement

*M*ost everyone is better at some things than others. Of course there are those rare individuals that make the rest of us sick.... they seem to be good at almost everything. Most guys out in the country are pretty handy at fixin' things out of just plain necessity.

Not old Harold..... he couldn't fix anything. I remember riding through his place lookin' for stray cows several times and seeing his old Minneapolis Moline tractor settin' there running, and he was no place around. If he shut 'er off he couldn't ever seem to get it started again, so he solved the problem. He hired a mechanic to come out and start it ever' spring, and then just left her running until fall.

Harold had other abilities, though. I'm convinced the Good Lord gives ever'body at least one talent.... hidden though it may be. My little woman is convinced that I've got the gift of discouragement, and

179

it dang shore ain't hidden, either. What a blow. And I'm such a nice guy, too.

Well, she'll be happy to know that I've turned over a new leaf. I've found a secret way to encourage the whole neighborhood, and by George it's workin'. Folks involved in this agriculture deal tend to be pretty down to earth pragmatic sort of people. Now, most of the time that's a very desirable trait, but it does have its shortcomings. When things go bad.... I mean really bad for a long, long time, a feller can get just plain depressed. After all, a guy can only take so much reality.

The good news is that it really doesn't take too much to cheer up a country boy. You might be surprised what an inch of rain can do for a guy's attitude.... even if he **REALLY** only got a half an inch. The truth sometimes hurts, so the idea here is to just alter the truth a little.

This plan of mine has worked wonders in encouraging this part of the world, and I'd like to try and persuade some of the rest of you to give it a try, too. I just carry my water jug around wherever I go and pour a little in every rain gauge I see. You don't even have to wait until a shower comes by.... a feller could starve to death doin' that. Nobody looks at the gauge until it rains anyway, so ever' one I see, I just pour in about an inch or so. You have to make this deal believable, so a guy really can't pour in too awful much.

I've never had so much fun in my life, and you ought to see the smiles. We had a little shower go through here a week or so ago, and I couldn't wait to ask the neighbors how much they'd gotten. They all know I don't have a rain gauge, so it's a perfectly logical question.

"How much rain 'd you get last night, Milt?" I asked, bitin' my lip to keep a straight face.

"An inch and three tenths," was the answer, "but boy she's dry. It didn't even make any puddles. She soaked right in the ground. That ought to do the grass some good," he grinned.

"Is that all you got. Milt?" asked ol' George. "I had an inch and a half."

"You're kiddin'," said a disgruntled Charlie, "we only got four tenths." (I never did make it to Charlie's last week.)

There was the proof I needed that I was really on to something. Those guys all got the same amount of rain, but two of 'em **THOUGHT** they got more than they really did, so they were happy as a couple hogs in a manure pile. Poor ol' Charlie knew the truth and was as grumpy as a bear with a sore butt.

"Success is right between yer ears.... scarey ain't it?"

The secret to survivin' and doing good in this ol' business of agriculture is right between your ears. It's mostly attitude. Grumpy ol' Charlie is the first one on my list for this week. I'll have to find an excuse to go over to his place and secretly doctor his gauge a little. The next time it showers and he really only gets three tenths he'll probably go buy a new pickup.

Boy... I didn't know that being encouragin' was so much fun.

Chapter Forty-Three

Two Tummie's Big Surprise

*T*here used to be an old German that lived over in the Yellow Pine country years ago. He was a bachelor and lived all alone up in the woods in a place they called Ramsey Gulch. He had a sawmill, and also logged for other mills around the country when his supply of boards got ahead of the demand.

A husky, red faced, hard workin' ol' guy, he was nearly as wide as he was tall. He always wore a pair of those big wide red suspenders to help keep his pants from fallin' down. A belt just couldn't get the job done. He was more than just a little paunchy... in fact, his belly was so big that when he got a couple of Blackfeet boys to help him up in the woods, they'd nicknamed him Two Tummies. Well, the handle stuck. I think his first name was Adolph, but a lot of folks in those parts didn't even know his real name. It was plain for ever'one to see that his new Indian name fit him perfectly.

Two Tummies was a master at the wood trade. If there was anything to know about the stuff, he knew it. He'd spent his whole life working with it in one form or another and just loved what he did. After a hard day at the mill or out in the woods, he'd spend his evenings out on the porch whittlin' something out of a pine knot. He could make just about anything.

It was back in the Thirty's sometime when he hatched his special "Christmas Plan". A simple man, he seemed to get by just fine without all the conveniences that most of the rest of the world would consider necessities. He was a robust, generous sort with a hearty laugh, and got the idea one year to make himself a Santa suit and visit some of the kids in the neighborhood. After all, he sure fit the part. He didn't even need a pillow, and with that fake beard he'd ordered from Sears and Roebuck, he could have fooled most anyone.

Now, reindeer were a real problem. Jiggs and Molly, his old Percheron work team would have to do. If any of the neighborhood kids ever recognized the familiar old grays as they plodded up the lane, they never let on. Most of the time he traveled in his old bobsled, but in the dry years he had to resort to the wagon.

He spent all year preparing for the special night. Even back in those hard times, Two Tummies was convinced that the real meaning of Christmas was somehow getting lost. So who better to tell the kids about the Christ child's birth than Santa Claus himself?

The long summer evenings were spent carvin' little shepherds and angels and all the other figures from the manger scene. Each one was different and unique. The pine knots made certain of that. He was a master at taking the unusual coloring and the different grain in each knot, and transforming them into a work of art.

A couple of days before Christmas, he'd make a trip into town, to pick up some oranges and apples and a few candy treats, and come the big Eve, he was all set to go. It got to be a regular tradition. The families up that way really didn't have too much, and the visit from Old Saint Nick was the best part of the entire holiday.

It went on for years. He'd start out just before dark, and get to the Wilson's just as they were gettin' done with supper. They were the closest neighbors, and he'd come in the door with his sleigh bells jinglin' and a hearty "Ho, Ho, Ho!" and begin to pass out the candy and other treats to the wide-eyed young 'ns.

It was something for the whole neighborhood to look forward to. At each house just before he'd leave, Two Tummies, (I mean Santa) would reach deep into his big sack and pull out one of his specially carved figurines, and tell the entire Christmas story to his eager audience. When he was finished, he'd leave the gift on the kitchen table, and with another "Ho, Ho, Ho!", out the door he'd go to the next house down the road.

As the years passed, every home in the neighborhood had collected almost the entire manger scene. Everyone would try to guess which carved figure Santa would bring, and Adolph was in his height 'n glory. He loved it.

One year something happened that changed the way a lot of folks look at Christmas. A big storm hit right after dinner that Christmas Eve, and by the middle of the afternoon, you couldn't see your hand in front of your face. It was the worst blizzard they'd ever had. Two Tummies was sick at heart, but there was just no way for him to make his annual rounds. He could barely get his front door open, and there were drifts at least six feet deep everywhere. His troubled mind was filled with pictures of the disappointed little faces he knew were waiting eagerly for him to come. He was certain all was lost.

He stoked up the old wood stove, resigned himself to the reality, and was just pouring a fresh cup of coffee, when in the door bounced the jolly old elf himself, shaking the fresh new snow from his bright red suit.

"Ho, Ho, Ho! Merry Christmas!"

Adolph's mouth dropped open in disbelief as the unexpected visitor placed a few treats on the table, then reached deep into his big brown sack, and as his host stood there speechless, drew out a perfect little lamb.... flawlessly carved from a Yellow Pine knot.

"I don't have time to tell you the whole story," he winked, "but I think you know it anyway. Ho, Ho, Ho! Merry Christmas!" He then vanished as quickly as he'd come. The next few days revealed the startling news. Every home in the entire neighborhood had received a similar visit, and they all had been left the very same gift..... a beautiful figurine of a baby lamb.... perfectly carved from a Yellow Pine knot.

They say there are some folks that claim they don't even believe in Santa Claus, but there's one thing I know for sure.... you certainly won't find anyone like that up on Yellow Pine.

Chapter Forty-Four

Lonesome Coulee Syndrome

The custom of coverin' the girls up with a veil like they do in the Middle East is something that I've been giving a little thought. Being an avid appreciator of the exquisite form and accoutrements of the fairer sex, the practice seems to me like a real travesty. After all, lookin' at pretty girls is about all the entertainment a poor boy like me can afford.

I think the custom must have been started by some poor Arabian cowboy with a whole tent full of ugly daughters. If you happen to be a poor ol' Dad, and your girls are good lookin' there isn't any problem. Hormones bein' what they are, you'll have 'em married off in no time. On the other hand if you've got a few bucks and the daughters are a little on the plain side, there still isn't any hitch. Money just seems to have a way of making them a lot prettier. A poor old man with ugly daughters is a bad combination.... he's just up the creek.

He and his not too gorgeous girls are really the only ones to benefit from this veil deal. Just think of the possibilities. If you're horse trader enough, you can tell all the young suitors that these gals are really hot stuff. "They're even better lookin' than their Mother, and boy she's somethin'." Of course she has a veil on too, so the poor victim doesn't know she's so ugly she'd have to sneak up on a glass of water.

After the marriage, it's too late. "A deal is a deal." The new groom sure isn't apt to tell the whole world he's just been slickered. In fact I'm certain, knowin' the male mind as I do, that he'd be braggin' up his new prize, and probably even telling his single buddies, "Yea, and the Old Man says that all those girls are even better lookin' than their Mother, and he says she's really somethin'. There's a couple more sisters over there.... you better check into it before someone else snatches 'em up." After all, what are friends for? Misery loves company, you know.

Mail order brides used to be sort of like that out west. Before telephones and pictures, neither party really knew just what kind of a deal they were gettin' into. There have been a lot of those kinds of arrangements through the years, but the scene has all changed now. These new computer matches give everyone a little better shot. You can talk to them on the phone and look at pictures, and assuming everyone is tellin' the truth, you've got a little more information available to make an intelligent decision.

That sure doesn't mean that everyone always uses their head when they make the choice, though. You take Bart Larson for instance. He and his new honey have stayed together for almost four years now, but they've got to be about the most mismatched pair I ever saw. Bart was sufferin' from what is known in these parts as "Lonesome Coulee Syndrome". It's a medical condition that only happens to bachelors that spend several years doin' their own cookin', washin' their own socks, and sleepin' all alone. I guess it's really bad stuff, and there just doesn't seem to be any cure.

Well, Bart got it. He was gettin' desperate. Somehow he got hooked up with this gal from California. He should've smelled a rat. She's about fifteen years younger than he is (which ain't all that bad), but she's one of those New Age meditatin' types that smokes roll-yer-owns. She grows the makins' out behind the house, so Bart didn't think too much about that, but he should have been suspicious when she only went by one name.... Moonbeam... didn't even have any last name, and to make things even worse she was a Democrat.

All those attributes in themselves wouldn't be so bad, except that Bart is a tee-totalin' Norwegian Lutheran that never voted for anyone that wasn't a Republican. They're as different as night and day, but after Bart drove the two hundred miles to get her off the plane, she looked so good in her jeans that he thought maybe he could overlook all the little things. Lonesome Coulee Syndrome strikes again.

They stopped off in town and got hitched right up and Bart and Moonbeam headed out to the ranch. She settled right in to the rural routine, and because they live at the end of the road, her runnin' around all summer in the buff didn't seem to bother the neighbors at all.

Politics seems to be their biggest difference. Moonbeam was good with the animals, and had a bucket calf that was always running around the yard. You know how they can be. He was constantly tryin' to get in the house and always seemed to need feeding.

"That durn calf must be a Democrat," quipped Bart one morning. "Looky there, he's always lookin' for a handout."

"No, I think he's definitely a Republican," answered Moonbeam, taking a long drag off her roll-yer-own. "Just look at that pot belly."

It was a constant battle, with each party bringing up the little bucket calf's most undesirable traits and blaming them on his adverse political connections. It all came to a head one summer day when the poor little orphan came up on the porch and started buttin' on the screen door.

"You know, I think you're right," Bart said thoughtfully gazin' through the screen. "That poor little bugger **must** be a Republican." Moonbeam perked right up, baskin' in her apparent victory, when her hubby continued,

"He'd never qualify for bein' a Democratic President.... the durn thing 's a steer."

"I'm not too sure that isn't against the law."

Chapter
Forty-Five

Brain Insurance

$\mathscr{D}$o you remember the Hollywood starlet that insured her legs for a million dollars a few years ago? I guess that her skirt must have accidentally gotten up over her knees a time or two in the filming, and she figured she was really on to something. She felt a need to protect her assets. You don't hear much about that kind of thing anymore.

It's probably because of the premiums. With all the hide they expose nowadays, the cost would probably be prohibitive. I've been thinkin' about insuring my brain. It really ain't fair that one guy should be so smart and good lookin' too. All things considered, I figure the premiums should be fairly low.

I've been doing some thinking about the whole Federal Land mess we find ourselves in, and have come up with an act for Congress to consider. It could be called The Federal Lands Distribution and Debt

Reduction Act. This plan is brilliant, if I must say so myself.

It's this kind of thinkin' that precipitates the need for brain insurance. The idea here is to get the BLM and US Forest Service Lands into the hands of individuals and onto the county tax rolls, while at the same time travelin' a little farther down the trail to fiscal responsibility. It probably wouldn't have a prayer of passage.... it just plain makes too much sense.

This proposal would put all Federal Lands, with the exception of National Parks and military and Indian reservations, up for bid. In order to be eligible to participate in the auction, the prospective bidders must be legal age individuals and US citizens. Everyone would have the same shot at a piece of the west.

Corporations or partnerships wouldn't qualify as legitimate bidders. The land would be auctioned, along with its attached mineral rights, in parcels of 320 acres on the courthouse steps of the counties in which they are located, and each individual would only qualify to purchase one parcel. It would be like the old homestead days all over again, except there wouldn't be any "provin' up" to get the free federal land. (I think the old timers will tell you that it dang shore wasn't free. They earned every dime of it.)

Let's face it, a lot of federal land really doesn't amount to very much, that's why it wasn't homesteaded a hundred years ago, but if it just brought ten bucks an acre, it would amount to over four and a half billion dollars. Some of it would bring a whole lot more. The money received would go directly into the Federal Treasury to help defray the national debt. The last time I looked, it stood at over five and a half trillion..... that amounts to over twenty thousand bucks per citizen. It would take a real bonehead not to see that everyone in the country would reap an obvious benefit. I purposely didn't write these numbers out....

it just takes too much ink. In the event that any parcel of land failed to receive a bid, the land would revert to the individual counties involved. Local control is always better.

The way I figure it, this would solve a whole lot of problems, and everyone stands to benefit. To say that the federal government hasn't been all that efficient in their management would be an understatement. The last figures I saw were from the mid nineties, and the net annual loss for the BLM and Forest Service at that time was over 350 million. I can't see any reason to let them dig the hole any deeper than it already is. The sales would also create an instant appraisal for the increased county tax base, and local officials might just have a little more money to help with the maintenance of the remote county roads.

Joe and Sally Rancher would have the opportunity to bid on a section of the land back behind the house that fits right into their operation, and Mr. and Mrs. Urbanite could buy themselves a piece of the American dream. Neither one would have to worry about some mogul or corporation buying the whole west, and then selling it to some oil sheik or turning it into a buffalo pasture. Of course if they wanted to raise buffalo or drill an oil well…. that's their business. After all, this is America.

Environmental concerns would simply disappear. There are those who will argue that individual owners don't have the brains to take care of their own property, and that the country is better off with the bureaucrats running things. I think their record in Washington, and ours out West shows otherwise.

Speakin' of taking care of things. I think I'd better get on the phone to the insurance man, before I have another idea.

"All those brainy ideas ain't helped us so much you'd notice."

Chapter Forty-Six

Bats & Boots

*T*hese cool evenin's sure do make for good sleepin' weather. The birds are evidently a lot smarter than some of the rest of us and pull the pin to points south. Bats head that way too, you know. That doesn't hurt my feelin's any. Our old house is nearin' the century mark, and we seem to get a couple in here every year. Fall always takes care of that little deal, though. We've pretty well got the windows taped up to where they can't get in them any more, but a few years ago they were a real pain in the neck.

The little suckers had decided that the attic of our old house was a nice dark place to spend the days takin' a nap before going out for a little bite to eat about dark. We could hear 'em floppin' around up there, and although that sort of puts you on edge, it isn't as bad as it gets....trust me. Some of them got a little disoriented or something, and wound up swoopin' around the house at night. There isn't anything that will cool off a romance like a bat in Mama's negligee. Until that happened, they were just a nuisance....now it's war.

I finally had the incentive I needed to really take the time to figure out where they were gettin' in. We found a spot where the old cedar shingles (nearly 100 years old, too) were missing out on the end of one gable. I got a hammer and some nails and an arm load of shingles, and gleefully plugged up their front door. We got 'em now.

One small problem....they were in takin' a snooze when I nailed their door shut, and now they're locked in the attic. About supper time they really started floppin' around up there. "Let 'em flop all they want," I says with an evil grin, "I'm gonna starve 'em to death."

Yea, right. Although there are probably several reasons I'm not entrusted with any nuclear secrets, the way my brain works is probably the first thing that would be a concern to the boys at the Pentagon. They started filterin' down out of the ceiling a little after supper time. At first it was sort of fun, but then we didn't have any idea what their battle plan was. That was just the first wave. After bed time they started gettin' really serious. Of course, they waited until we were sound asleep before they attacked in force.

It was a sneak attack. The first one that dived bombed our bed, the little woman pulled the covers over her head, and ordered me out. "Get that thing out of here!!" I guess she figured one bat in her nightgown was enough. We had a couple of teenage guys here helpin' with the hayin', and I rousted them out to help. We used various weapons, from brooms to window screens, but the weapon of choice seemed to be a tennis racket. There were bats everywhere, and me and the boys were yellin' and swingin' like our lives depended on it.

Then we heard this gigglin'. It was sort of faint at first, but it steadily got louder. Dodgin' a couple of hungry kamikaze bats, I discovered the source. It was the ol' lady with one eyeball sticking out from under the covers. She seemed to think that a dozen divin' bats engaged in a pitched battle with three hyperactive cowboys dressed in nothin' but their Stetsons and their skivys was about the funniest thing she'd ever seen. In her opinion we put the Three Stooges to shame.

I don't give up easy. OK, so I'm stubborn, but after two days I surrendered. My wife and children were gone and the two ranch hands were threatenin' to quit. Mama had pulled out and told me she wasn't comin' home until I "fixed it." So I reluctantly got the ladder and my hammer and went back up and opened the hole back up in the roof. That ended the problem....it was "fixed", at least temporarily.

We got a big Chinook wind along in January, and I climbed back up and patched the roof again while the bats were on their annual Southern sabbatical....but this time I locked 'em out instead of in. I hear there are folks that sleep with a gun by their bed. There's a tennis racket by ours.

Excuse me.... that must be the Pentagon calling.

Ol' Cannibal

I got this little pony fer my Mother-In-Law
Some say I done it fer spite
But he's gentle.... really..... an' easy to ketch
..... a little hard to turn to the right

Ol' Cannibal's what we call him
He's nice and quick on his feet
Raw hamburger's the best way to ketch him
He shore likes the taste of fresh meat

Chapter Forty-Seven

Slim MacDonald's Last Ride

*T*he name his Mama had given him was Duncan Angus MacDonald, but ever'one just called him Slim..... he was tall and sort of skinny in his younger days, I s'pose that's why. He had a little place down on Two Calf Creek a few miles from where it dumped into the Missouri. Boy, that's a rough chunk of country. They say that range is so rough that the magpies will bust their wings just tryin' to fly over it.

You've got to be a hardy sort and a dang good cowboy to even survive in that neck of the woods, and Slim seemed to do quite well. His wife had died when she was rather young, and poor ol' Slim had gone it alone down there for years. Being a thrifty Scot, I think he had the first nickel he ever made, but he did a couple of things that were just plain out of character. One of them was that he played a good hand of poker. Now, that's unusual for a guy that's close with his money, but Slim was among the best. The other thing he did to everyone's surprise was to buy the highest priced casket that was ever sold in these parts. I overheard him recounting the reasons for his uncharacteristic extravagance at the county fair a few years ago.

"It all started one evenin' in roundup camp, and we all got to singin' like we used to do to pass the time, and we had sung up about ever' song we knew. Then Charlie Parker struck out on "Battle Hymn of the Republic".... man, we musta been gettin' desperate for material. There's that one line in there, "John Brown's body lies a moulderin' in the grave...." Boy, now that got me to thinkin', and the thought of Duncan Angus MacDonald doin' any moulderin' didn't sit too well with me, so I went out and bought the best restin' box I could find."

He had 'er shipped in all the way from Chicago. It was made of copper and lead, and had a big brass eagle on the lid. The durn thing weighed over 500 pounds. The dray man liked to hurt himself haulin' it from the depot. It also featured a big thick triple rubber seal. Slim was bound and determined not to do any "moulderin'".

Time went on, and the poor ol' boy got himself busted up pretty bad in a horse wreck, and had to move into town. That seemed just fine to him, because the poker partners were pretty few and far between out on the creek. The rheumatism set in somethin' awful, and it got to where he couldn't even straighten up. He was all bent over in a number 7 when he walked. Of course when he sat down, you couldn't hardly tell, and seein' he was down at the Bucket o' Blood playin' cards most all the time anyway, he got along just fine. He never missed a game.

Well, as fate would have it, pneumonia got him down one winter just after Christmas, and the poor ol' boy passed on over the "Great Divide." He had a ton of friends, and ever'body missed him, but the undertaker was presented with a couple of rather unique problems. The first was that he had to round up six of the biggest honkers in the county just to carry Slim and his now famous casket, but the second problem proved to be even more of a challenge.

When he laid the ol' boy out in the box, his feet stuck straight in the air, and when he pushed his feet down his head would come back up. Slim's joints had plumb given up to the rheumatism, and his poor ol' body was just froze that way. Nothin' he tried worked, until he got the bright idea to screw a couple of D rings off an old saddle into each end of the bottom of that high priced lead box. He used Slim's own lariat rope to slowly apply pressure to both ends of the thrifty old gent, and after several hours he had him all stretched out flat. He just dressed him up in his Sunday suit to cover up the rope across his chest, and he looked purty as you please.

Four of the Kaliwalski boys and the Olson twins finally got him loaded in the old hearse, and after pumpin' up the tires a little bit, they started on their way slowly down Main Street with a long procession of mourners in tow. Sean McLean was to go in the lead with his bagpipes, and although it was so cold and windy he was afraid his kilt would freeze, he marched out bravely in the front playin' an old Scottish dirge. The streets were just a glaze of ice, and it was snowin' hard along with the cold north wind.

They were just a couple of blocks from the funeral parlor when there was an awful wreck. Some new guy from California was drivin' the produce truck on a delivery to the grocery store, and had never driven on streets that slick before. He just couldn't get 'er stopped, and plowed that big truck right smack into the side of the hearse. The truck made a connection right behind the hearse's back wheel, and she spun around in the street until she was headed right back the way they'd come. They smashed into a light post

201

and Slim and his high priced casket squirted right out the back and headed down the street.... straight for the Bucket o' Blood. It was a downhill run, and he musta been travelin' at least thirty miles an hour when he hit the front door.

Now, the boys at the poker table in the rear were just observin' a moment of silence as they heard the bagpipe approaching. It was the least they could do.... bein' good friends and all. Their eyes was still shut when over seven hundred pounds of lead and copper crashed through the front door. Slim and that high dollar Chicago casket cut a pretty wide swath down through the bar, just freight trainin' everything in their path, and smashed into the concrete wall in the back of the room, coming to rest right beside the round green table with the four would be mourners.

It was an awful crash. The impact busted open the casket lid, and ripped out the D rings that had been installed to hold poor ol' Slim in a horizontal position. The rheumatism strain on those old joints must have been somethin', for when the pressure was released much to everyone's surprise and shock, he sat right straight up, and sent the old Stetson hat that had been placed on his chest spinnin' through the air.

Everyone was in complete shock, not knowin' if they should stay or make tracks out of there...... that is ever'one but Ol' Sam, the town drunk. He was sittin' at the end of the bar with little bubbles risin' from under his hat, and had watched the whole show in slow motion. There was a long eerie silence then Sam spoke up,

"Don't jusssht ssssit there. Deal th' poor guy in. I tol-ja Shlim couldn't passssh up a game."

Chapter Forty-Eight

Granny & The Twelve Gauge

My Grandma Overcast came from the Ozark Mountains. As soon as the television series "The Beverly Hillbillies" started, she was dubbed Granny, and carried the handle until she died. If you remember Granny from the TV show, then you have a purty good picture of my Granny, too.

She was definitely from the old school. Granny always wore a dress. Somehow the idea of wearin' pants plainly didn't sit right with her. She just didn't think that it was the proper thing for a lady to do. Oh, she'd wear pants when it was cold or when she was outside workin', but it was always under her dress and her apron. That way she could just pull the jeans off and change her apron when she came back in from feedin' the chickens or doin' the chores.

She was ever' bit as spry as the TV Granny, too. Whatever needed doin' outside she could get 'er done.... dress, apron, jeans and all. There was the ever-present toothpick in the corner of her mouth, and her outdoor wardrobe was never complete without her favorite fishin' hat. She was a real prize.

I think it was a bad ear infection when she was just a kid that caused her to wear the hearin' aid. It was a big old contraption about the size and weight of a box of 30-30 shells with a wire runnin' from the control box up to the deal that she stuck in her ear. The wire ran down her neck and into the top of her dress. The Good Lord only knows where she hooked the big control box, but it was way down in there someplace. The poor ol' gal was plumb deaf with out it.

My Grandad was gettin' a little feeble, and called me one mornin' to ask me if I'd help Granny pick up a few potatoes. He wasn't up to it, and they had just bought some potatoes from one of the neighbors that needed pickin' up out of the field that day. We arranged a time to meet in the neighbor's spud field, and they already had a row or two dug with the potato digger when I got there.

Granny tied into that row of potatoes like she was killin' snakes. Do you realize how humiliating it is to have your eighty-year-old Granny out work you? I had to pick spuds like my life depended on it just to try and keep up.... passin' her was out of the question.

She was always game for anything. Whatever job needed to be done, she'd just tie right into it. Such was the case the time we were havin' trouble with blackbirds in the sweet corn patch. Dad had some good sandy ground down by the Milk River, and had planted three or four acres of sweet corn. Having a whole house full of juvenile indentured servants like he did, Dad was convinced that teachin' us what sweat tasted like would be good for us. There's nothing like draggin' a gunnysack full of sweet corn around 'til you have a truckload to help build the old muscles, you know... not to mention your character.

Well, the blackbirds were just wreckin' the patch. We tried everything. Scarecrows were a joke. The birds just built a nest in his hat. Granny absolutely couldn't stand for anything to go to waste, so she volunteered to keep watch.

"I'll betcha I can stop 'em," she declared.

Armed with an old Winchester twelve gauge shotgun, Granny was on the job at daylight ever' morning. You could hear her blastin' away clear up at the house. The explosions were a little hard on her ears though, so she had to turn her hearin' aid off.... leavin' her deaf as a post. She'd hit the ones she could, but found it almost as effective to just fire away indiscriminately into the air. After a few of their kin folk had been blasted out of the sky, just the sound of Granny pumpin' in another round was enough to scatter the rest of the flock.

It was upon this scene that happened a salesman one fine August day. He was a smooth lookin' dude with patent leather shoes and a big Oldsmobile with power windows. I guess he was probably lookin' for Dad, and followed the noise out into the corn patch. He suddenly came face to face with what by all appearances was a deranged old lady.... just blastin' away into the air at nuthin'. Her corn patch wardrobe was probably more than a little eccentric looking to a stranger, and to make matters even worse, she didn't hear him comin', so didn't answer when he called out to her.

KERBLAM! KERBLAM! "That 'll teach ye!" Granny cackled. **KERBLAM!**

"Oh, 'scuse me Sonny. I kain't hear ye. Just a minute," she said as she reached deep into the recesses of her dress to plug the wire back in on her hearin' aid. "Nice day, ain't it?" **KERBLAM!**

205

" . . . . 'Scuse me Mister."

I'm sure he felt his life was nearly over, and escape was the only thing on his mind. "S-Sorry Ma'am. I m-must be lost. I was just l-leavin'!" stammered the foiled salesman as he pointed the roarin' Oldsmobile for anywhere but there.

We've never seen him since. It's sure too bad ol' Granny's gone. I'll betcha we could rent her out as a salesman control officer.

Chapter Forty-Nine

Keep Yer Socks On

There are a few things that seem to stay the same in this world of rapid change. It used to be said that this part of the country was only fit for "steers and bachelors, and it was dang hard on women and horses". There have been a lot of improvements in the last hundred years or so that have made it a lot easier on the last two categories, but there still seems to be a bachelor or two out in the hills. Apparently they like it that way, but personally, I'd never make it. I'd starve plumb to death.

A lot of the bachelors I know are sort of bashful around girls. At least they are until they get a few drinks under their belt, and then no self-respectin' gal would be caught dead with 'em. Booze has a strange way of turnin' some of the nicest guys into something just plain uncivilized.

Steve Oiestad is a bachelor friend of mine. He's kind of a handsome devil too, but so far has been able

207

to twart the advances of the many ladies that would like to make his acquaintance on a little higher plain. I've never seen him drink too much, so liquid courage doesn't seem to apply in his case, and bein' naturally bashful has really put a damper on any potential romance.

He is one heck of an artist too, and will probably be as famous as Charlie Russell someday.... unfortunately it might be after he's been dead awhile. That's sort of how that art stuff works. An artist's cash flow is about as certain as a cowboy's, and sometimes the light bill needs payin' **BEFORE** someone decides they can't live without your latest masterpiece. That's how he got in this jam.

A few years ago there was a Hollywood movie company filming a picture up in the Wolf Creek Canyon or someplace over that way, and they hired Steve to do some painting on a few of the sets. With his talent the job was a breeze, and they were very impressed with his work. Unfortunately (or fortunately, depending on your perspective) the female star of the movie was quite taken with this strong, handsome, single, Montana cowboy.

She was a real dish, too.... about the best lookin' thing to cross the mountains in a long time. Half the guys in Montana would have given their right arm to be in Steve's predicament. Not only was she gorgeous, but she was rich, too. Now, that's a real bad combination for a naturally bashful guy.

The set painting job didn't last but a day or two, and the sultry young actress was increasingly frustrated by the fact that she couldn't seem to gain the attention of her intended male victim. (I'll call her Cindy. It's not her real name, but I wouldn't want to embarrass her.) She was of course accustomed to all the men just falling at her feet, and Steve seemed completely oblivious to her charm and beauty. Nothing she tried seemed to work.... until she hatched a devious plan that was certain to draw him into her web.

"I've been admiring your talent," she cooed one afternoon, "you are really very good."

"Thank you, Ma'am," Steve answered, not looking up from his work.

"I would like to commission you to paint my portrait. What would your fee be?" She obviously knew that the key to an artist's heart is through his pocket book.

"I'll give it some thought," Steve answered in his most non-committal tone, "but my schedule is fairly tight, right now." Actually the only thing on his schedule was to feed the dog.

Not to be brushed away so easily (no pun intended), Cindy went on. "I'll pay you twenty-five thousand dollars, but it will have to be done while we're here on location. I'm scheduled to fly to Italy the end of the month for another picture."

"Whoa!" Steve thought to himself, "Now that's a real chunk of change. I've finally hit the big time!" He was suddenly a lot more interested in visiting with her than he had been just a minute before.

"Of course," Cindy continued as alluringly as possible, "it would have to be a very **SPECIAL** portrait.... I'd like you to paint it in the nude."

This caught my bashful bachelor friend a little off guard, and he stammered his way through an embarrassed reply, concluding that he would have to think it over. He promised to check his schedule, and give her an answer when he returned the next day. She was certain his foot was in the trap now, and that he was at long last firmly in her clutches.

The next day dawned, with Steve struggling to arrive at the difficult decision. He of course had to weigh all of the moral factors against the obvious financial realities, and had finally come to the conclusion that he'd go ahead and do it. Cindy was waiting with anticipation as he stopped by her trailer on the film location.

"I've rechecked my schedule, and I can fit in time to complete your commission. And," Steve continued haltingly, "I've decided to agree to your wish to paint it in the nude." With Cindy's passion now definitely on the rise he continued, "but you're gonna have to let me leave my socks on 'cause I need someplace to wipe my brush."

Some guys are just cut out to be bachelors.

Chapter Fifty

Sparkplug & Whiskey Dick

*I*t seems like every one of these little rural communities has a local character or two, and some of those boys can sure be entertaining. A lot of 'em hit the bottle a bit too hard, and most of them are more than just a little short upstairs. A very disturbing thought came to me last week. A friend of mine pointed out that our little community was gettin' a little shy in the character department, and suggested that maybe I needed to fill in, you know.... do my part.... bein's as most everyone views me as a little eccentric, and all. (Charlie Russell said that's just a polite way of sayin' that yer nuts.) Because I'm not a real excessive bottle tipper, I guess it ain't too hard to figure why he thinks I'd qualify.

There used to be a real character that lived close to a little town down the road a ways. They called him Whiskey Dick. You really didn't have to be around him too long until you figured out why. Nobody knows what kind of a guy he'd be if he was sober, 'cause he never was. He was certainly entertaining, though. I guess he'd been quite a cow puncher in his day, but that day had long since past.

He used to drive that same old floppy fenderd '49 Ford pickup into town almost everyday. He had a regular stool in the Stockman Bar... at least when it was nasty outside, and sat on a slice off an old Cottonwood log on the south side of the building when it was nice. Everyone in town looked out for him, and gave him a lot of room when they saw him and that old pickup comin', but one day he and the old jalopy got into an altercation with a light post, and the Judge took his driver's license away. For the next few months, he drove an old McCormick Deering tractor to town, but they finally had to put a stop to that, too.... he was just gettin' too dangerous. That's when he started ridin' old Sparkplug in from the country. Who knows what his real name was, but he was even more of a has-been than Whiskey Dick, so that's what ever'one in town called the old nag.

Dick was a cowboy to the end. You'd never see him without his hat and boots, and always had his rope on his saddle, and a pair of old batwing chaps thrown over the horn. "You never know when yer gonna need 'em," as he would say. He'd ride into town and just drop ol' Sparkplug's reins on the ground next to the Cottonwood stump, and go in for a little nip or two. That old horse never moved. When Dick would sit outside, he'd use the old pony to block the summer sun.... he'd just pull him a little one way or the other so that his perch there on the stump was always in the shade.

It was on to this real live western scene that happened a couple of eastern tourists one hot August afternoon. Larry and Melvin were as excited as can be to find a real Montana cowboy and his faithful steed,

212

and ol' Whiskey kept them entertained for most of an hour with his wild stories of life out on the plains. After a while, one of the pair wandered off down the street a ways to take in a few more of the sights, while the other sat enthralled at Dick's feet.... believin' ever' word of the most outrageous BS you ever heard. Finally, fearing that it was getting late, Larry asked Whiskey Dick if he had a watch.

"What fer?"

"I need to know what time it is."

"I ain't never seen the need for a watch, but I can tell you what time it is." With that, Dick leaned over and pulled ol' Sparkplug's tail off to the side, and gazed up between his hind legs for a while.

"It's dang near Three-Thirty," answered Whiskey Dick. Now, that was the most incredible thing that Larry had ever seen, and he ran down the street to tell his friend what had just happened. He caught up to him just in front of the hardware store.

"What time is it, Melvin?" he asked breathlessly as Melvin glanced at his wristwatch.

"Three-Thirty."

"I knew it! These cowboys are absolutely unbelievable! They have lived out on the prairie alone for so long that they don't even need a watch to tell the time!" He went on to relate the amazing story of how this national treasure of a real cowboy they'd just found could tell the time just by lookin' at his horse's rear end. Of course, Melvin was a little hard to convince that even a crusty old puncher like Whiskey Dick was so in tune with nature that he could tell time to the minute just by gazing up between a horse's hind legs, so they decided to kill another hour or so, and go back to test the old cowboy's ability again.

Time seemed to drag. They were both anxious to see this real live miracle happen right before their eyes again. Not wanting to make Dick suspicious that they were testing him, they agreed to just visit about a few other things first, and then casually ask what time it was. Melvin really needed to see this for himself. He hid his wristwatch in his pocket, and soon the time had come to pop the question.

"Boy, it's getting late," says Melvin, "what time is it Dick?" Whiskey Dick leaned a little forward, just as he'd done before, and pulled ol' Sparkplug's tail off to the side, and after a long squinty gaze between his hind legs, answered.

"A quarter to Five." Melvin pulled his watch out of his pocket, and sure as shootin', Whiskey Dick was right on the money.

"See, I told you!" Larry blurted out. Melvin was flabbergasted.

"How in the world did you ever learn to tell the time just by looking under your horse's tail? This is the most amazing thing I've ever seen!"

"It takes years of practice," Dick answered seriously, with little whiskey bubbles coming from under his hat. He then spit out a big wad of snooze, and continued, "You gotta have yer head in just the right spot."

"Yea, Yea," said Melvin impatiently, anxious to master this new found frontier technique. "Right spot for what?"

"You gotta twist yer neck down like this," Dick demonstrated as he pulled Sparkplug's tail off to the side again. "Then when you get ever'thing in just the right spot, you just look right up here between his legs.... an' you can see the clock on the bank."

Chapter Fifty-One

Speed Dial Baloney

I'm not sure if all of this progress stuff is really progress. How come all of these inventions to make our life easier get harder to figure out all the time? I think maybe I've finally discovered where I officially fit as far as a political label is concerned. I must be a "Progressive Regressionist". At least I guess that's what you'd call a guy that is goin' backwards a little faster ever' day.

The older I get the more I think all this new-fangled stuff is a bunch of baloney. In fact if there's ever a movement of radical regressionists formed, they'd probably want to make me their president. After all, I'd make a wager that I have the newest outhouse in the state..... well, maybe I won't bet on it... the durn thing must be a couple of years old already.

Now, just take Oral for instance. His ol' lady came home from town with a new-fangled telephone the other day that had one of those "speed dial" features, and it almost got him gunned down in his own kitchen. It was awful.

She read all through the little book that came with it, and it wasn't too long until she had 911 and the Doctor's office, her sister, her mother, the Vet, a few of the neighbors, and a half a dozen other numbers all programmed into it. All you had to do was punch one little button. The dang thing starts beepin' like it's gone crazy, and before you know it, you've got the other party on the phone. Boy, now this even sounds like progress to me.

His little woman tries it right out, and shows Oral some of the finer points. "See right here where it says Doctor.... just push that button, and it rings right into his office." In fact, she was going to go in for a few tests, as she hadn't been feeling too well, and was planning to call in to confirm the appointment. She even had Oral push the button to prove to him that it would really work.... he can be kind of a bonehead when it comes to this 'lectric stuff.

"Well, I'll be doggoned," says the ol' fella as the nurse answers the phone. "Here," he says as he hands the phone to his wife to make the arrangements. It worked just like a top. "Ain't technology wonderful?"

I guess it was just a coincidence, but Oral's old saddle mare had been goin' downhill pretty bad, and as long as his wife had to make a trip into town anyway, he thought maybe he'd just load her up and haul her into the Vet to see if he could do anything for her. As soon as the little woman was done talkin' to the Doctor, Oral brimming with his new found knowledge, puts on his readin' glasses and punches the button marked "Vet". Sure enough, it rings right through, and he makes arrangements to take the old mare in the next day.

They get all loaded up and he drops the wife off at the Doctor's office and then heads out to the Vet with ol' Flossy. She's thirty-four years old, so there isn't too much the Vet thought he could do, but he did give her a little something that would hopefully keep her insides workin' a little better. "If you happen to be in town tomorrow, bring her by and we'll check her out again to see if this is doing any good." Oral agreed, and swung back by the Doctor's office to pick up the little woman.

As fate would have it, Wifey had to come back in the very next day to get the test results from the Doctor, so Oral figured he'd just run the mare back in again with the same trip. So far.... so good.

Come the next mornin', after a jaunt to the barn, my friend figures out it isn't any use. Ol' Flossy is worse.... not better, and he resigns himself to the fact that he's going to lose her. Not being able to stand seein' her suffer, he digs out his old Winchester, and begins to steel himself to get the nerve to carry out the lousiest job any cowboy can have. He just doesn't have any choice.

Right after breakfast as the little woman is getting ready to run in for her test results, Oral makes the final decision that hauling the poor old mare to town is futile, so decides to call the Vet to let him know that he isn't coming in. One little problem.... he forgets his glasses, and punches the wrong button, and gets the Doctor's office by mistake. He thinks the Vet sounds a little hoarse, but then he's been known to get in the sauce on occasion, and after all it is early.

"Doc, I won't be bringin' that old girl in this mornin'."

"Is there a problem?"

"Problem? I should say so. What ever you did to her yesterday sure didn't do her any good. As a matter of fact she's quite a bit worse. I really hate to, but I guess I'll just have to shoot her. She's been a dandy too, but she is getting along in years, and I can't see pourin' good money after bad. I'm afraid she's gonna

217

get down and not be able to get back up. Besides, one of the neighbors just brought a couple of good lookin' young fillies up from Utah, and I think I'll see if I can't talk him out of one of 'em. I don't know what he thinks he needs two of 'em for anyway. Boy, they're really built, too."

The doctor excitedly motions for one of the nurses to call the authorities on another line as he tries to talk some sense into an obviously deranged man and buy a little time in the process.

"I think you should bring her on in. I won't charge you anything to examine her a little more extensively. I'm certain we can get to the heart of the problem."

"Naw, thanks anyway Doc, but at her age I think Dr. Winchester is my best bet. I've got my mind made up.... it's hopeless; I just as well shoot the old girl and get it over with. Thanks for lookin' at her, and go ahead and send the bill on out for what I owe you. Bye."

Wifey comes out of the bedroom, hairbrush in hand, and wondering what all that noise is. **WHUP! WHUP! WHUP! WHUP!**

"That sounds like a helicopter! And look outside! It looks like the Army is after us! Quick, Oral.... do something!" One quick glance out the window confirmed their greatest nightmare. The yard was full of a bunch of commando lookin' guys with machine guns and bulletproof vests.

"Quick, Mama! It must be the ATF and the FBI! Get under the table!" shouts Oral as he pushes the refrigerator in front of the door and reaches for his ol' Winchester. "First Randy Weaver... now us! I ain't goin' down without a fight!!"

"Oral Elser! This is the Sheriff! Come out with your hands up!"

"Sheriff??? Ma, it ain't the Feds.... it's only Bob Cunningham, the new Sheriff," Oral says with a sigh. "I wonder what in the world has got into him?"

218

After a few tense moments they finally got things resolved. The riddle was at long last solved in time to avert a tragedy. Everyone had a good laugh, and Oral tore out that dad-blamed new phone and put the old one back in. He's going to make a great candidate for President of the "Progressive Regressionist Party", don't you think?

Chapter Fifty-Two

Aunt Ethyl & The Gravy Ladle

*J*oey Markel's aunt Ethyl was a real piece of work. Although all us kids thought she was just "it", we sure didn't look forward to her greetings. She was one of those cheek-pinchin', hug you till you die, Grandma kind of gals.

To say Aunt Ethyl was a big woman would be an understatement. Huge would be a lot better word, and unless you took a real deep breath before she grabbed you for one of her famous smother hugs, you were a goner. She'd completely bury your head in the soft front of that blue flowerdy dress of her's, and you were sure you were gonna die before she turned you loose. It was just like gettin' swallowed by a feather bed. I think her perfume must have come from Monkey Ward's in a five-gallon can.... but she made the best peanut butter cookies in the whole world.

Her and Joey's Uncle Ralph never had any kids of their own, but they'd taken Joey in to raise when he'd lost both his folks in a car accident. It seemed like they'd adopted all the rest of us kids in the neighborhood too, and those peanut butter cookies were sure worth the huggin' torture we had to go through to get them.

They made sure that Joey went off to college in Bozeman, and were proud as punch of his grades. He was a good kid, and studied hard. That's why it wasn't a real big surprise when Aunt Ethyl got the call early in the fall quarter of his junior year.

"Aunt Ethyl, I had to move out of the dorm. Those crazy guys over there are carryin' on and making noise all hours of the night, and I can't get any studying done. But don't worry, I found an apartment, and I've got a roommate. It's not going to cost any more than it did to live in the dorm, and it'll sure be easier to study for all these tests."

"Oh, honey," Aunt Ethyl replied, "that sounds like it's going to work out a whole lot better. We're sure looking forward to you coming home for Thanksgiving. Is your car running OK?"

"Yea, the car's fine," Joey went on, "but I won't be able to make it home for Thanksgiving this year. I'm taking an extra credit class, and so I'm just not going to be able to get away."

"That's fine Dear, you know best. Your Uncle Ralph wants to go hunting anyway, so I'll just come down and cook you dinner at your place. I'll be there on Wednesday evening," Auntie concluded as she hung up the phone.

Sure enough, come the Wednesday evening before Thanksgiving, Aunt Ethyl's blue Buick pulls up in front of Joey's apartment. She had the backseat piled high with goodies that she'd been cookin' for a week. She was sure that Joey's roommate was probably a big eater just like he was, and she wanted to make sure she had plenty of food. "Growing boys need to eat," she always said. She met her little Joey with her famous "smother hug", but then nearly lost her false teeth when she met the roommate. She was a cute little trick, and her name was Jennifer.

Now Aunt Ethyl was from the old school. This cohabitation stuff wasn't even in her vocabulary. It was totally out of the question. Joey explained to her that Jennifer was just his roommate.... that's all. She had her end of the house, and he had his.

"It truly isn't safe for a lady to live alone in this day and age, and besides," Joey went on, "she does a lot of things around the house that are really natural and easy for a girl to do.... it works out great for everyone."

Aunt Ethyl was a little on the naïve side, but she didn't just fall off a turnip truck. She really wasn't buyin' Joey's sales job. It could have had something to do with the way she caught him looking at Jennifer.... kinda like a hound dog looks at a pork chop. The two days she spent there were a little strained, but Joey kept trying desperately to convince her that everything was above board. "She's just my roommate.... that's all. There are lots of arrangements like this nowadays." When his Aunt Ethyl loaded into the Buick for home, he really wasn't sure if he'd convinced her or not. He wanted her and Uncle Ralph to be proud of him, but after all he was a big boy now.

Then a strange thing happened. About a week or so later, something came up missing. Jennifer had a silver gravy ladle that had been her Grandmother's, and she couldn't find it anywhere. "The last time I saw it, was when your Aunt Ethyl was drying the dishes on Thanksgiving," said Jennifer. "She and I were talking about it, and I told her how much it meant to me, and she was really admiring it. You don't suppose she would have taken it, do you?"

"Aunt Ethyl? Naw, of course not. It must be around here someplace." They tore the kitchen apart, but couldn't find it anywhere. Although Joey was certain that she would never take anything, with Jennifer's urging he finally wrote a letter home.

"Dear Aunt Ethyl, I'm not saying you took the gravy ladle, and I'm not saying you didn't take the gravy ladle. What I am saying is, the last time we saw it was when you were drying the dishes and admiring it. We've looked high and low for it, and Jennifer is just heartsick that it's lost. She wanted me to write and ask you about it. Love, Joey." A week later he received a reply.

"Dear Joey, I'm not saying you're sleeping with Jennifer, and I'm not saying you're not sleeping with Jennifer. What I am saying is, that if Jennifer was sleeping in her own bed like you told me she was, she'd have found that gravy ladle by now."

It's purty hard to get one over on Aunt Ethyl.

Chapter
Fifty-Three

The Reflection

Like most ever'one else that has a love for the west, I'm a real Charlie Russell fan. I stumbled across an old book contain' some of his pictures and stories in the dump a few years ago. What a treasure. I can't imagine, for the life of me, why anyone in their right mind would throw somethin' like that away.

The best part of all was that it was edited by one of his contemporaries. Some crusty old gent had corrected a lot of the text, and written very colorfully all over the margins. I suppose the ol' guy had died and whoever was cleanin' up his stuff just didn't see any value in an old book full of scribblin'. What I wouldn't give to know who it had belonged to and then be able to talk to him myself.

I've gotten a little insight into some of the bigger things in life thanks to ol' Charlie's pictures. Did you ever notice that in a lot of the scenes he painted of the main streets of our little towns, there is usually an old Red man in a blanket backed up against a wall? I had really never given that a whole lot of thought. In the pictures that come to my mind, the old Indian is never the focus of the painting, but rather just a fact of life.

He was just one little piece of the picture; a rather nonessential part of society. If he hadn't been there, the painting might have lacked authenticity, but it's doubtful he would have been missed all that much at the time. The look on his face was often rather blank, but his eyes would reveal the feeling in his heart; a mixture of contempt and hopelessness and anger. They seemed to say, "Why don't you just go away and leave us alone."

I travel around quite a bit singin' cowboy songs, and tellin' stories, and a year or so ago somethin' happened that made me go back and look at a couple of those old pictures again. I was in another State at a big cowboy music doin's out in the middle of no place. It was a real old cowboy town. Although there were a couple of newer buildings, the main street was pretty much the same as it had been for a hundred years, with old false fronted stores lining both sides.

It was just before noon on a Sunday mornin', and a cup of coffee sounded good, so the cook and I decided to take a little stroll to find one. There were people everywhere. Everyone was in town to see the big show. We finally found a place that had some coffee, and after a while managed to get the strange lookin' dude in the hair net to understand we just wanted coffee. No fu-fu juice, no tootie-fruity....just coffee. He charged us an arm and a leg, but we finally got our plain coffee, and headed back up the street.

The old buildings that were once the lifeblood of this little ranchin' community were enough to make you cry. What was once the saddle shop now sold tie dyed t-shirts, and imported rugs, and the old hardware store didn't even have any hardware, but instead

226

was runnin' over with sweet smellin' candles and all sorts of typical tourist trap junk.

We sat down on a bench to finish our coffee, and watch the people go by. They were a sight for sore eyes. A lot of 'em were in floppy sandals and bermuda shorts, but some of the others were dressed up in their best cowboy suits. Do you remember how Bob Hope looked as a cowboy? The only difference was he was **TRYIN'** to look funny.

That's when it hit me. Here I am a real cowboy in a real old cowboy town, and I don't fit. I was a square peg in a round hole, and I didn't like the feelin'. The place had been taken over by a bunch of foreigners. Urbanites. They talk different, they dress funny, and they don't understand our ways. Just then I turned and caught my own reflection in the store front window.

There it was. I'd seen that look before. The expression on that face could only be described as blank, but the eyes revealed the feeling in my heart; a mixture of contempt and hopelessness and anger. They seemed to say, "Why don't you just go away and leave us alone." But as in the old Red man's time, they ain't goin' anywhere. They're here to stay.

Finally, ...I understand.

Thanks for comin' along. We hope you enjoyed your ride through the Real West. Remember ....

Keep Smilin' ....

     and don't forget to check yer cinch.

Ken

"... and there was the house, under a hill
by a barn made out of log"

The Mist of the Wild Rose

We rented some range a few years back
It was quite a ways away from our own
And come the fall, we're a few head short
So I was checkin' to see where they'd gone

Now there's a big lease that lay just to the east
Of the place where our critters had run
So I saddled early One September mornin'
Headed into the risin' sun

It was one of those perfect kind of a mornin's
The air was fresh and clean
The chokecherry leaves wore a special red
Like somethin' out of a dream

231

I must have ridden and hour or two
Without givin' my pony a rest
when we came to the top of this long old ridge
So we paused for a while on the crest

Streched out before us lay this deep wide valley
With an old set of buildin's by a spring
I always get such a lonesome feelin'
When I run into that kind of a thing

Nobody 'd lived there for many a day
Maybe fifty years or so
And I got to thinkin' about the hopes and dreams
Of that family from so long ago

Well, I pointed Ol' Red down off that hill
Completely forgetin' the strays
Gonna check out this outfit from out of the past
Just an old set of buildin's today

Now there was a foggy kind of a mist
                    Between the buildin's and me
I really didn't pay it no mind
It's common here that time of year
We're travelin' easy, takin' our time

But this was different
Than any I'd rode through before
It smelled like a million wild roses
Like ridin' through Heaven's own door

It didn't last but a minute or two
And it was clear on the other side
But by the scene that stretched out
                              before me I knew
This wasn't no ever'day ride

For there was the house, under a hill
By a barn made out of log
But there was a boy, 'bout four or five I'd guess
And he's playin' with this old Shephed dog

"Now somethin's playin' tricks on my mind,"
                              I thought.
"I know nobody lived there."
I'd just checked it out from the top of the hill
The whole place had needed repair

But now every shingle was in it's place
And the barn wasn't needin' a door
It was plain as day there were people around
Not at all like it looked before

I hollared "Good Mornin'" as I neared the gate
But the boy didn't answer my call
Neither he nor the dog paid me no mind
....Like I wasn't there at all

"Good mornin', Sonny," I called again.
But the boy just continued his play
Well, maybe he's deaf, I thought to myself
But why don't that dog look my way?

I tied my pony there to a post
And walked up to the open door
"Anybody home?" I asked the lady inside
But the response was the same as before

Her stove was black and shiney
And a calendar hung there on the wall
1897 Year of our Lord
No wonder they didn't answer my call

Now I could see them, but they couldn't see me
If that ain't a strange kind of a twist
Somehow I'd managed to ride through time
It had somethin' to do.... with that mist

I pulled off my hat and stepped inside
Just tryin' to take it all in
There was a Mama puttin' bread in her stove
And a boy outside with his friend

She was hummin' there in her kitchen
As she busied herself with her chore
A little baby was doin some fussin'
In an old apple box on the floor

"Hush little Sarah now don't you cry
Daddy be home bye and bye
Hush little Sarah now don't you cry
Daddy be home bye and bye"

I guess it's my reward for wonderin'
For always wantin' to know
But here I am in this old house
And it's a hundred years ago

I made my way to a corner
And sat down there out of the way
I can still smell that bread bakin'
And hear that baby fussin' today

But the aroma of that bread was soon smothered
And million wild roses blew in
On a breeze through the open doorway
The mist, and the roses.... and the wind

It was all over in less than a blink
And I sat in the corner alone
The Mama, her babies, and that old Shepherd dog
In one single heartbeat were gone

Her stove lay there in a rusty heap
The curtains no windows or panes
What once was a home just a breath ago
Now just lonely remains

I sat there alone and I pondered
On all the things I'd just seen
The home that was then, and the loneliness now
And such a fine line in between

But my time of reflection was shortened
'Cause there behind an old door
I caught the glimmer of silver
Comin' from a crack in the floor

I couldn't believe my good fortune
A silver dollar I pulled from its grave
For some reason they must have forgotten
That old cartwheel they put there to save

It bore a Carson City mark
The year was Eighteen-Eighty-Nine
It'd spent all those years under the floor
That brand new dollar of mine

Well, I shoved my treasure down in my jeans
As into my saddle I swung
My mind was swimmin' with the pictures
Of when this country was young

I pointed Ol' Red up out of that yard
Still thinkin' on things of the past
To a little knoll up behind the house
One that I nearly rode past

And there on the crest sittin' lonely
With only the sky for a friend
One single slab of sandstone
Stood there on its end

I couldn't make out the inscription
It was nearly lost there in the Buffalo grass
Just a solitary sentinel there
To guard a life from the past

So I steped off and bent down to read it
And this is all that it said
"Year of our Lord, Ninety-Seven
Baby Sarah, Pneumonia" it read

I could hardly contain my emotion
I'd seen her just one minute before
Right down there in that kitchen
In that old apple box on the floor

I lost all track of time after that
Searchin' my heart and my soul
And lookin' down on that old set of buildin's
I spent the rest of the day on that knoll

Now if somethin' 'bout this sounds familiar
And you go back home to check up on your own
Baby Sarah still sleeps there in the Buffalo grass
And your dollar?
      ......it's under her stone

Ken Overcast Recordings

Montana Campfire
Cowboy Stories and Songs

Woopie Ti-Yi-Yo, More 'n One Way to Skin a Cat, The Tail of Two Traders, Old Shep, The Million Dollar Invention, Hot Dang, To Bill or Not to Bill, Tyin' Knots in the Devils's Tail, Sellin' on the Street, Buck 'n Bertha, The Tattoo Lady, The Cowboy's Prayer

This is our latest, and what fun it was.

Thinkin' Back
One of Our Most Popular Titles

Cow Creek, Thinkin' Back, Ghost Riders in the Sky, How to Be a Man, A Cowboy and His Bride, Supper Time, Life is A Song, Younger Yesterdays,   Master's Call, Rockin' Alone (In an old rockin' chair)

One of our most popular. A couple of these were singled, and got a lot of play in Europe.

Live!
A Great Time!

Who Needs You, Younger Yesterdays, Tequila Sunrise, Night Rider's Lament, The Cowboy Song, Dumas Walker, A Cowboy and His Bride, Memphis, Ghost Riders In The Sky, I Left My Heart In San Francisco, Move A Mountain

There is about as much variety here as you'll find. We flew a crew in from LA and this is what they got.

Prairie Poetry, Vol 1
Grammy Nomintated Poetry

Kamikaze Mama, The Cowboy & The Queen, The Old Diamond O, Arnie Ain't A Cowboy, Home, Damned Old Hole, Arnie's Fuzzy Face, Grandma's Gown, The Propane Story, A Cowboy's Christmas Prayer, The Mist of The Wild Rose

This one is all poetry, and has gotten a lot of recognition. It includes the classic, "Mist of the Wild Rose".

Montana Cowboy
All Acoustic Cowboy Music

Cold, Broke, & Hungry, Ride Cowboy Ride, Blizzard, Workin' Cowboy, Montana Lullaby, Back in the Saddle, What's it Take To Make A Cowboy Cry, When the Work's all Done This Fall, Cattle Call, Mr. Shorty, Ridin' Down The Canyon

This is one of my favorites. It's just me, a Montana cowboy....yodelin' and all.

Ken & Karlie
Daddy/Daughter Duo

Broken Dreams, Dad (Today I'm Comin' Home), Country Girl, Grandma's Gown, Mama Likes My Cowboy, Faded Love, The Eagles Still fly, Don't Take Me Home, You Can Be A Cowboy, Move A Mountain

Daughter Karlie does a great job on this one. We have a great time together, but she's home bein' a Mama.

Silver & Gold
All Gospel / All Original

Got My Ticket, Set Your Mind, Goin' To Heaven, Silver & Gold, Rock And Redeemer, I Will Restore, Granny's Mansion, Across The Great Divide, Foot Of The Cross

I wrote all of these while in some deep water. If you need a little encouragement...this is the one.

www.kenovercast.com
or
Call Toll Free
1-888-753-7611

Discounts available for bulk purchases

About The Author

Ken Overcast is a Montana cowboy. Although he's gained national recognition on several occasions for his entertaining performances and writing, "just bein' a cowboy" is his real first love.

He and his wife Dawn have raised their kids on the ranch which lies on the banks of Lodge Creek in north central Montana. Their country life style is all they've ever known, and they wouldn't trade it for the world. Ken claims to both "raise and dispense B.S.", and Dawn says that, "he's always running off someplace or other to play that darn guitar and leaving me home to do all the work." It's that very attitude of finding humor in everyday life that has greatly contributed to the entertainment career of this real Montana cowboy.

Ken hosts a nationally syndicated radio program (*The Cowboy Show*) and has also written and recorded several CDs of music, stories and poetry. He is the recipient of the coveted *Will Rogers Award* from the *Academy of Western Artists*, and his *Montana Cowboy* CD received the prestigious *Best of the West Award* from *True West Magazine*.

240